BETTER NEVER THAN LATE

BETTER NEVER THAN LATE

Chika Unigwe

Abuja - London

First published in 2019 by Cassava Republic Press

Abuja—London

First published in the USA in 2020 by Cassava Republic Press

A CIP catalogue record for this book is available from the National Library of Nigeria and the British Library.

ISBN 978-1-911115-54-0
eISBN 978-1-911115-56-4

Book design by Seyi Adegoke
Cover & Art Direction by Seyi Adegoke
Printed and bound in Great Britain by Bell & Bain Ltd., Glasgow

Distributed in Nigeria by Yellow Danfo
Distributed in the UK by Central Books Ltd.
Distributed in the US by Consortium Book Sales & Distribution

For my goddaughter, Ekanem Akwaugo Nkechi Okeke, who is smart and fierce: may you continue to soar. Fly high, the sun will not melt your wings.

For my young nieces, Zite, Ayanachi and Bianna Unigwe: may you inherit a world that will never succeed in shrinking you.

Table of Contents

The Transfiguration of Rapu

The new man was tall and lanky, his stomach not spilling over his trousers like those of the other men who gathered at Prosperous and Agu's. Yet, despite that, he moved in such a way that put Prosperous in mind of an overfed, pampered cat. He had a fashionable haircut and a thin strip of beard in the middle of his chin. This was a man for whom life in Europe had not been hard. Prosperous envied him that; a life untouched still by hardness, soft like a baby's buttocks, like the life she had lived before.

'My beautiful wife, Rapu.' A small woman suddenly appeared from behind him. She sat down on the edge of the sofa as if she were ready to flee at the slightest sound. When Prosperous asked if she wanted a drink, she nodded but did not specify what, not even when Prosperous asked, 'Mineral or juice?' She held the glass of juice Prosperous gave her with both hands, as if holding it down to keep it from flying away. She was new. But not in the same way the man—Gwachi—was. She was new to Europe. He was just new to Belgium, and to the group that met regularly at Agu's to drink and talk, dissecting their lives and sharing their nostalgia for a country they swore they could not wait to live in again, once the money was made and they could retire and live in the mansions they were going to build in Lagos, Abuja, Enugu, Onitsha, Jos. Whichever city in Nigeria their deferred lives still inhabited.

The new man had moved from Germany a few months ago, Agu told Prosperous the first time Gwachi visited with his paper-wife, his German wife, Hilde. 'He said Germany is very hard for black men. Harder than Belgium. Can you imagine? Hilde suggested the move to Turnhout when he said he had heard this place was easier for blacks. She gave up her life in Germany for him. Oyibo women and love! They'd give up everything for the person they love!'

Prosperous did not remind him that there was a time when he would have given up everything for her. And she would have done the same for him—did do the same for him. Prosperous said instead, 'We have all given up things.'

The wife Gwachi had with him now, and whom he brought most times he came afterwards, and with whom he had a six-year-old back in Nigeria, was Igbo, like everyone else in the flat. Rapu did not live with him. She lived with a Nigerian man called Shylock. Nobody seemed to know what his real name was. He had earned his nickname for the exorbitant fees he charged for whatever service he provided, even to his fellow Igbo. Shylock drove an Audi, had a gold tooth and always wore a beret and dark Ray-Bans. In the winter he wore a long black leather jacket with a furry trim on the hood.

At Christmas, he threw lavish parties where the signature dish was Chicken Shylock, a succulent affair that exploded in a multitude of flavours in the mouth, sour and sweet, spicy and soothing mint. No matter how much anyone begged for the recipe, he refused to give up its secret. It was said that he threw even bigger parties in his village at Easter where he gave out bags of rice and tins of palm oil to widows.

Gwachi complained that Shylock was charging him too much. 'Twenty thousand euros! And we are from the same village, the man is my kporakpo! He loves money too much, when am I going to pay all that off?'

'You make it sound like you're paying off a car,' Prosperous said, irritated.

'Shylock is expensive, but he never dips into a pot of soup that is not his,' Agu said.

'You remember the story about that Ogwashi man?'

'What ha-ha-happened to the-the...the Ogwashi man?' Rapu asked.

The Ogwashi man had been paid a huge amount to marry a certain Ogwashi woman whose husband was already in the country but who could not bring her in because he was legally married to a Belgian woman. The man—very much like Gwachi—missed his "real" wife so much he did not want to wait until he had got his papers and divorced his white wife to bring her in himself. But the Ogwashi man not only took the money, he also took the wife—even going back to Ogwashi to pay her dowry once the husband in Belgium had had his dowry returned.

No one in Agu and Prosperous's circle of friends knew who the Ogwashi man was but his story had become an anecdote, told and retold in their circle to warn each other of the covetous nature of human beings. Shylock, whatever else he might be, had an untarnished reputation for honesty and professionalism. If he said he'd sell you his mother, he would, was how he was described. He was also a man with lots of connections. No one knew the exact nature of those connections, not even his kporakpo, his village-man, Gwachi, but they were said to be expansive and useful. He was the sort of middleman you wanted if you were after an "arrangee" marriage. He would know whom you could trust.

As it turned out, when Gwachi asked if he could recommend someone, Shylock said he would go one better. So, Gwachi paid for him to go to Nigeria and marry Rapu in court. 'He even charged me for the suit he wore for the ceremony!' Gwachi complained to Agu and Prosperous. He went to Shylock's every evening after work to see Rapu briefly. On Sunday afternoons or evenings, he made excuses to Hilde, and went to see Rapu. It was only then that he took Rapu out like a proper husband and they went and visited his friends, or drove down to Antwerp where they checked into cheap hotels and kept an eye on the clock while they made love. It would not do to make Hilde suspicious.

'How long still?' Rapu asked every night when he dropped her off at Shylock's.

'Not long now', came the standard reply.

Rapu told Prosperous all this when she visited.

'What does theee... theee... this woman look like, my hus-hus-husband's wife?' Rapu asked Prosperous one day, her voice low and soft, her eyes dull. She was sitting on a kitchen stool, stirring her plate of rice and stew listlessly with a spoon.

'I've only ever seen her once,' Prosperous lied. 'Gwachi does not go out with her much. He brought her here once.' Then, because she knew what this woman, the real wife, wanted to hear, she added, 'It's almost as if he were ashamed of her. She's muscular, yams on her legs and arms! She's not beautiful. She has a beard like a man's own. Gwachi should ask her to shave.'

Prosperous felt guilty but she squashed it. What good would it do tell Gwachi that Hilde was beautiful? Long black hair that contrasted sharply with her pale skin, pleasant manners, youthful looks. She looked like an advert for healthy skin. Or to tell her that Hilde and Gwachi held hands like children when they visited, that they touched each other when they spoke, finished each other's sentences? It was much kinder to lie.

Rapu's lips turned upwards in a smile. Her eyes brightened. Very softly, she said, 'Thank you.' She did not stutter.

At a party in Lier a few weeks later, Rapu danced towards Prosperous, hips twisting, nothing of the nervous-looking woman, the johnny-just-come newly arrived in Europe, in her, and dragged Prosperous to the floor. 'My hus-band doesn't... doesn't want to dance. Wasting the music.'

She moved with a flexibility that Prosperous envied

and she told her so. 'Ah, it he-helps with the stiffness, dancing. Shy-Shy-Shylock's sofa is not a comfortable bed!'

She snapped her fingers to the music, leapt into a backward shuffle, threw her hands in the air and shrieked in delight as another song began to play. Prosperous danced opposite her. Rapu had to shout to be heard.

'First Gwa-Gwachi was in Lebanon. Then Ho... Ho... Holland. Then Germany. Now he says hee-hee-hee-he's settled. Once he divorces Hee... Hilde, and I divorce Shylock, we'll be too... too... together again. I'm tired of sleeping on the-the-the sofa. My neck hurts. Every day. Another man might have given the woman the bed but not Shylock.'

'Oh well, Shylock doesn't joke. It's always strictly business with him. If he gave up his bed for you, he wouldn't be Shylock. That's why your husband trusts him. No funny business with him. You know where you stand.'

For two weeks, Gwachi did not visit. Instead Rapu came with Shylock. 'I beh-beh-begged him to bring me,' she told Prosperous. 'Gwachi and Hilde ha-have gone to Turkey on holiday. To-to-together.' She sounded like she was about to cry or had been crying. The hip-throwing, finger-snapping woman at the party had been usurped by this nervous-looking one.

'She sleeps with my hus-hus-husband every night. She's got him and what ha... ha... have I got?' She wrung her hands as she spoke, cracked her knuckles.

'In a way, he is her husband too,' Prosperous said

gently. She usually tried to avoid thinking of the woman with the delightful high laugh whom Gwachi brought along to theirs sometimes, though not as often as he brought Rapu. The woman had mock-complained once that rather than taking her to Nigeria to see his home country and meet his people, Gwachi was taking her on a tour of Nigerian homes in Belgium. 'It's not the same, you know darling?' Laughing in that high way of hers, kissing him on the nose.

'Tell her,' Gwachi had said, appealing to the room. 'Tell her how dangerous Nigeria is. It's not a country to visit. It's not like Kenya or South Africa where you can go on safaris. Why do you think I left? Ah, tell her about our country!'

Prosperous had said nothing, unwilling to be dragged into the performance expected of them, demanded by friendship. But Agu and Godwin had complied. They magnified Nigeria's flaws, transforming it with their words into a nation with none of the redeeming features they spoke warmly of over plates of eba and soup *(Food tastes so much better in Nigeria! In Nigeria, people might not have much but they are always willing to help! Nigerians are so much happier than these oyibo people! Our people are resilient! Resourceful! Brilliant! The best ever!)* and that they defended when Agu talked of how some 'ignorant man at work who has never even been on an aeroplane' dared to ask if Nigerians lived in trees *(Imagine! He doesn't know that Nigeria is a rich country! We export oil!)*. They spoke to Hilde, instead, of kidnappings at gunpoint; of policemen who sold their uniforms and rifles to armed robbers; of constant power outages and air so thick with the exhaust fumes of rickety old cars that it was impossible to breathe.

As they piled one horror story on top of another, Hilde's smile became thinner and thinner, almost disappearing into her face. When she shrieked, 'I never want to go to Nigeria! What a horrible country!' Prosperous left the room.

Later, when real terror came to Nigeria—daily bombings in the north-east, abductions of schoolgirls, entire towns being razed, Fulani herdsmen terrorising citizens—Prosperous remembered the stories these men had told and wondered if somehow by focusing on all the negatives, by exaggerating those, they had birthed these new horrors.

When Gwachi returned from Turkey at the end of August, his visits with Rapu continued. He had bought her a small leather bag, which Rapu showed off happily. 'How was your holiday?' Prosperous asked him.

'What is there to do on holiday?' He played with Rapu's braids, ran a palm over her back. 'I missed my wife. Hilde wanted to see museums. To shop. To walk. Every morning, she dragged me out to walk.' Gwachi's voice, however, remained soft, a feather, a voice wholly lacking in conviction. Prosperous wondered if she was the only one who caught it.

'Walk to where?' Agu asked, laughing in anticipation of the response.

'To nowhere! Just white people's walk. Hand in hand. Like schoolchildren.' He sounded sad, wistful. His laughter accompanying Agu's loud one rang hollow.

Rapu shook his hand off her back and walked away into the kitchen. Prosperous followed.

'You know I kept asking heee... him to bring me. Bring me over. Bring me, I said, I can hah... han-handle it. I missed him. Now, I don't know. Maybe I should ha... ha... have remained in Nigeria.'

A few months later, Rapu came to visit Prosperous. She was on her own. Her lipstick looked like it had been hastily put on. Her eyes were red. Prosperous thought someone had died.

'What's wrong, Rapu?'

'Heee... She... Hilde is—'

'She's what?'

'Pregnant!'

It was the first time Prosperous had ever seen Rapu cry. She had seen her close to tears several times and had imagined that, if she eventually did cry, it would be soft sobs with lots of sniffing. But Rapu moaned when she cried, a ghost in a Nollywood movie.

'He won't lee... lee... leave her now, my sister, will he?'

'Is that what he's said?'

'No. No. But he... he... he... ' The words refused to dislodge and she gave up and wept into her palms.

'You know Hilde is pregnant?' Prosperous asked Agu later. He did. 'Is he going to abandon her with a baby? After everything she's done for him?' She felt like throwing something, flinging a cup at the door, smashing a window, anything to ease the anger building up in her.

'Rapu is his wife, is she not? She's the one who's recognised back home. She's the one we recognise, the one who has his child already. He'll do right by Hilde. But his marriage to Rapu, that's the one he needs to fix.'

'But Hilde?' Prosperous said, not quite sure what she wanted to say.

'You want him to leave Rapu and his son for her?'

'This is just fucked up,' she said.

Two days later Prosperous ran into Gwachi and Hilde opposite the baby shop on Gasthuisstraat. 'We're going to set up our baby registry,' Hilde told her. Gwachi stood beside her, his eyes shining as if he had been shown some wonder. Prosperous recognized the look of pride. She muttered 'Congratulations,' and walked off.

It was Prosperous who noticed that Rapu was gaining weight. She joked to Gwachi that Shylock was feeding his wife well.

'It's this-this-country,' Rapu said. 'Too many sugary things to-to-to eat.' She took a large bite of the cake Prosperous had served and sipped some Coke. Her eyes had lost their startled look and acquired a certain calm. When she spoke, she no longer wrung her hands or cracked her knuckles. She settled into Prosperous's sofa as if she owned the place. She asked for music so she could dance. She no longer mentioned Hilde or her pregnancy.

'Her eyes are opening,' Prosperous said to Agu. She liked this woman.

Rapu picked up weight steadily so that whenever Prosperous saw her she had piled on more. The weight was spread evenly over her body, as if it had taken a conscious decision to be fair. One day, Rapu told Prosperous she was pregnant.

'And what does Gwachi think of it?'

'He-he-he is happy,' she said, burying her head in her glass of Coke as if she were afraid of looking Prosperous in the eye. 'Two babies at once! He-he's happy.'

'Gwachi doesn't know how he's going to deal with it,' Agu told Prosperous later that night. 'Two babies coming in the same year. He thinks it'd be very cruel to leave Hilde now she's almost due. He loves Rapu but he also loves Hilde. He said that her parents were totally against her marrying a black man. She married him against their will and her father is still not talking to her. She hopes that the grandchild will help bring her parents round.'

Prosperous thought of Hilde fighting her parents for the man she loved. She thought of Rapu and her growing stomach. She thought of Nkonye in Nigeria, waiting to join his parents. She did not know whom to feel sorry for, whom to root for: Hilde or Rapu?

In May, as the weather became warmer, Hilde had her baby. A girl with her father's nose, bigger than the average baby girl. She was fifty-four centimetres at birth, Hilde announced proudly as she handed the baby over to Prosperous when she and Agu visited. 'Guhwashi has been very good with her,' she said. 'He hasn't dropped her once!' Her laughter filled the room.

'Ah, me, I'm good with babies,' Gwachi responded, taking the baby who was now sleeping from Prosperous and putting her down in her cot. His delight in his baby puffed out his body so that his stomach looked rounded, as if he too had just gone through a pregnancy. His eyes shone with a familiar intensity. She wondered now if he and Rapu would set up a baby registry too. She and Agu, as well as many of their Nigerian friends, had not been very generous with the gifts they chose from the list for this baby with her father's nose: rattles and hair brushes and feeding bottles and baby nail clippers. They were saving up for the *real* wife's baby.

'When Rapu *drops*, we'll buy the pram!' Agu boasted to Gwachi in Igbo as he handed over the plastic rattle he and Prosperous had brought. He had already levied some of their friends 50 euros each to buy a *Pericles* like Princess Mathilde's baby had. 'Nothing but the best for our baby!'

Gwachi had laughed and thanked them but Prosperous thought the laughter held something else, something weightier, something less carefree. Prosperous did not mind spending so much money, almost 800 euros on a pram, but it bothered her that they acted as if Rapu's baby was the real baby, and Hilde's own some impostor they had to pretend to care for until Rapu's arrived.

'*Guwashi* is like a pro. You wouldn't tell that this is his first. He impressed the nurses at the hospital,' Hilde said. Gwachi smiled and kissed Hilde on the forehead. He asked her if she wanted something else to drink; her tea had got cold.

Prosperous watched Gwachi fuss over Hilde, holding her hands and kissing her repeatedly on the back of one hand, and she wondered if his exaggerated kindness was him loving her or compensation for the fact that he would soon be leaving her. He no longer spent Sunday evenings with Rapu. He had to be on hand, Rapu told Prosperous, to help out with the baby.

'He-hee-he says once the baby is three... three months old, he'll leave her.' Rapu sounded like she no longer cared.

One Friday morning in July, Rapu came to visit Prosperous. It was the first time she had come on a weekday. Agu was out and Rapu looked relieved to hear that.

'My sister. I don't want you to hear... to-to-to hear this from someone else. So I'll tell you. My baby's father is not my husband.'

Her baby's father? What was she talking about? Prosperous thought of Shylock's untarnished reputation. She thought of how everyone respected his sense of integrity. 'Shylock?'

'Shylock? No!' Rapu shuddered as if the thought itself repulsed her, and then laughed with her entire body, her merriment pouring forth into the room. 'I met someone. I loh... love him. So now Gwachi can keep his oyibo wife.'

'Does Gwachi know?'

Rapu shook her head. 'I'm not a bad person, you know? But I'm only hu... human. I tried. Every time I asked Gwachi how-how much lon-lon-longer it w-would be, he-he would tell me, "Soon. I don't want to be cruel to her. She ha-ha-has been very good, very good to-very good to me."'

Prosperous said nothing and so Rapu said, 'I'll tell

him. I'll tell him and then I'll lee... lee... leave him. He
won't be too sad my sister. He does not loo-loo-look too
unhappy with Hee... Hilde.'

Telling Prosperous must have been her trial run for
telling Gwachi. 'Today, I'll tell him,' she said, running
out as if she feared she would lose her resolve if she
stayed any longer.

Rapu was already out the door before Prosperous,
stunned into silence, got her voice back to ask who the
father was, to ask who Rapu was leaving Gwachi for. She
worried for Rapu. What would people say? How brave,
though, she thought. How freeing it must be not to care
what anybody thought, not to mind losing the close-knit
community she had built up here, because who would
still be seen with Rapu once the story became public?

'I've got news,' Agu shouted jubilantly, coming in
almost as soon as Rapu left. If he were a dog, Prosperous
thought, his tail would be wagging. Her own news could
wait. 'Gwachi has asked Hilde for a divorce. Today! He's
on his way now, as we speak, to give Rapu the good news!'

Finding Faith

This was one of the reasons Oge did not like to shop at this time of year: too many people, too much noise. Her hands were full, and she wondered at how very difficult it had been for her to make her selections; the tyranny of choice, she thought wryly. Many more hands would be useful. She struggled to hang onto the huge racing car with one hand while she picked up the plastic bag containing the Transformer, which had somehow slipped from her grasp.

She had thought it would be fun to have a baby born close to Christmas, and used to tell Jordi what a lucky boy he was: three celebrations (and therefore three sets of presents) in one month: Sinterklaas on the sixth of December, birthday on the seventeenth, and Christmas on the twenty-fifth. *Who's the luckiest kid alive?* she'd ask. *Me! Me! Me!* Jordi would reply. But shopping for presents was always a chore. The shops were full of people. The year Jordi turned two, she had tried to shop earlier to beat the holiday traffic but realised that many toyshops held off discounts until the beginning of December. At the prices they charged, Oge preferred to wait for the sales.

Jordi had been planned, wanted and excitedly expected.

All over the flat, signs of that expectation sprouted like mushrooms. Oge would go to bed and wake up to a new pram that Gunter had bought. Or Gunter would come in from a walk around the neighbourhood and find a teddy bear Oge had picked up. There was no concern then about the astronomical prices. Only the best for the baby who had already been named in utero by Gunter. Oge had preferred to wait until he was out to give him his middle name. An Igbo name, which her parents called him. Okwukwe. Trust. Faith. She could not name a child while it was still on its journey to the world, she told Gunter. You had to wait for that journey to end, to hold the baby in your arms and then find a name that summed up the totality of the experience from the pregnancy to the birth. A name that would suit, rather than burden a child. She told him of the friend of a friend of a friend in Enugu who named her daughter Beauty. But no one could call that baby Beauty with a straight face!

Jordi had asked for a Transformer last year for his fifth birthday, and she had said no. Put her foot down. Been a strict parent. *There's no way I am paying that much for such a fragile thing!* And all for what? Now she wished she had given in, given him the one toy he swore was going to make him the *happiest boy ever in the whole wide world, Mommy!* She remembered dragging him out of this same shop, telling him off for crying because she had said no. *You are so spoilt, Jordi! And for that I swear to you, I'll never ever buy you a Transformer.* How proud she was of herself then, of how she had refused to give in to a five-year-old's tantrum in a shop full of other shoppers watching. When she recounted the story to Gunter—who often accused her of being the more easily manipulated parent—she was again filled with pride. She thought of herself then as a parent who could be both firm and fun. *One day, when you're all grown, you'll thank me for this,* she had told Jordi.

She almost abandoned her haul at the counter—a racing car with lights that blinked, a police car with a plastic cop inside it, a set of finger puppets, a Lego train set—when she saw running around in the shop, the way Jordi had once, a child of about the same age, curls like tendrils falling over his eyes the way Jordi's tended to. At the beginning, she had seen Jordi everywhere she looked. Children whose features dissolved through her tears when she took a closer look and saw that they could not possibly be her son, there was no resemblance at all! She could not stand to be in the shop, watching the child who looked like Jordi appear and disappear through the aisles like a magic trick, but her resolve to get something for him won. Faith wins over fear, her pastor was fond of saying. Faith is steadfast. She had believed him.

The weather was starting to grow cold. Outside, Christmas decorations hung above the street. How Jordi had enjoyed being out at this time of year, enthralled by the sparkles and the lights. His first Christmas, she and Gunter had taken him to the town square to witness the installation of a Christmas tree as high as a house. The cold air brushed her cheeks but she felt a sharp pain in her throat, burning like an open wound with pepper rubbed in it; an ulcer of the throat.

If you have faith as small as a mustard seed, you will say to this mountain, Move! And it shall move. The mountain will pick up and run! How many times had the pastor said this? Ministering to her over and over again. *Faith is free. All you have to do is accept it. Accept faith and be healed.*

Back in Nigeria, and even here in Belgium before her life fell apart, she had had faith. It had come easily to her. In her first months in Belgium, when she suffered panic attacks and worried that she would never learn enough of the language to get a good job, this language with its aspirated g's and solid r's, her faith had seen her through. When, in her fourth month of pregnancy, she began to spot and feared she was losing her baby, her faith had seen her through. When Jordi appeared, healthy and beautiful after a long labour, filling the delivery room with his enthusiastic cries, his name had come to her. This, she thought, was the fruit of her faith. But when she needed it most—after Jordi's accident, when she and Gunter began to argue and bicker and sleep in different rooms—her faith had been nowhere to be seen.

Bereft. Jordi's accident had hollowed her out. It had scooped out her insides like the flesh of an avocado. When the phone call came from his school, she had been getting ready to pick him up. She still had her lipstick in her hand when the phone rang and the school nurse, whose voice she recognised (Jordi had his share of scrapes at school), said, *Sorry, there has been an accident, Jordi is in an ambulance on his way to the hospital.* He had never needed an ambulance before, so that fact in itself had panicked Oge. She had jumped into her car and driven to Sint-Elisabeth Ziekenhuis, not even thinking to send a a message to Gunter.

Jordi will like what I have chosen, his presents from Sinterklaas, but only now did she remember that she also wanted to get him a pack of cards. No way was she going to return to the store. She was still shaken by the image of the boy who could have passed for Jordi. The cards would have been a good addition. A reminder of happier times. In the old days, she, Gunter and Jordi would sit around every evening playing cards, laughing at the faces they pulled at each other, everything as it should be. One happy family. She felt the burning in her throat again. She should have made a list. She was always forgetting things. Gunter used to find it endearing. *My forgetful wife* he used to say, laughing. *My forgetful wife. One day you'll forget your head. And then where will we all be?* And she had laughed with him too. If anyone had asked her then to describe her marriage, she would have said it was one endless laugh. There were times in that previous life when she thought that she should have named her son Songoli. An excess of joy. For everything their life was.

She had bought too many presents. Gunter always scolded her for spoiling Jordi. In their one-long-laugh marriage, this was the only point on which they disagreed. *Children don't need expensive presents,* Gunter would say. *You know how many mouths that can feed in Africa?* She used to argue with him, tell him the only people with a social conscience were those who were brought up on plenty. *I want my son to have everything I never had.*

But it doesn't have to be expensive. Think about how much that is in naira.

No. I won't do that conversion because it doesn't make sense. Are you going to stop buying beer because, whenever you convert how much you pay for it, it comes to lots of naira? Or your fancy wine?

But today, if he were around, she would have no strength to argue with him. There were more important things on her mind. She still had to bake Jordi's cake. Carefully mould the fondant stars and moon to go on it. Last year, Jordi wanted to help, getting under her feet as she baked. She shouted at him, said if he did not leave the kitchen, she would not bake his cake at all. Of course she had not meant it. Bereft and regret. Two words that complement each other. She was bereft, hollowed out, and where her flesh should be were regrets. Where her Okwukwe should be was empty. *What has happened has happened,* her father had said to her only days ago. *What is important is what happens now.*

She had arrived too late at the hospital. A nurse had taken her to a room, flooded in light and the stench of antiseptic, and asked if there was anyone they could call. Oge had given Gunter's number and asked if the nurse could take her to see her son. She had not understood the look on the nurse's round face, nor had she understood when she said kindly, *Let's wait for his father to come. The doctor will be with you soon. Would you like some tea, some water?*

Six months it had been now. Six months to the day since first Gunter and then the doctor had come into the room, and the doctor said, *We did all we could. It was really a freak accident.* She did not understand, not immediately, but Gunter held his head in his hands and bawled like a child, and Oge rubbed his back, trying to get him to stop.

It was later, much later—after the doctor and the police and the school headmaster had spoken to her and gone—that her brain was able to reassemble all their words into some sort of terrifying coherence. Jordi had been playing on the monkey bars in the school playground when his body became wedged between the bars. His ribcage was pressed tight and his lungs couldn't fill with oxygen. How was it that she remembered these details? When she slept, she often had nightmares where she saw his feet dangling. She woke up every day and it still seemed impossible that Jordi was dead. That he would not grow to be the pimply hormonal boy who would break hearts.

Gunter used to joke in the beginning that he was jealous of Jordi. *My son has taken over and now you have eyes only for him.* To prove that this was not true, she would make love to him and later they would both stand over Jordi's crib and marvel at the beautiful creature they had made. They delighted in sharing titbits of what he had done, what he had said. His smile.

Did you see that? He just smiled at me!

I don't think so. I think that was gas.

No, it was definitely a smile. You're just jealous. Jordi said Dada today!

No, he said Mama!

No way. Dada. I heard him loud and clear. Da! Da!

There had been delight in their conversation, before. In the four long days leading up to the funeral, Oge stayed in bed, too numb to deal with the details. But that was no excuse, she told her father later when she could speak of it, for Gunter to have him cremated. *I am Igbo. We don't do cremations!*

He doesn't know that, her father said, *coming to Gunter's defence. I am sure he did not mean to hurt you. You should talk to him, Oge.*

Just before Jordi was born, Gunter was on a train that derailed, killing two passengers. He escaped without even a scratch. Yet Oge had spent days afterwards crying, not from relief, but for the tragedy that might have been. *I could never imagine being without you,* she would often say and he would respond, *And neither could I.* She thought then that the worst thing that could happen to her would be losing him. That had been her biggest fear. That Gunter would die. In an accident. From an illness. From age (way in the future). And she would be left alone. Jordi would be both her comfort and the child she would have to console. The one who would be left behind when she went too. Faith outlives everything, she had believed.

At the coffee table after the funeral service, when mourners filed into the restaurant of the crematorium, murmuring in low tones, filling the tables piled with ham and sandwiches and liver pâté and jugs of orange juice and shiny pots of tea and coffee, all she could think of was the impossibility of Jordi being dead and the cruel coldness of this send-off. She had watched the crematorium waiters in black, looking like undertakers, walking silently among the guests, asking *Would you like water?* and *Shall I pour you some tea?*

At Gunter's grandfather's funeral years ago—her introduction to a Belgian funeral—the whole thing had seemed odd to her. Nobody cried, at least not loudly, in church. It did not matter that the man was almost ninety; in Nigeria, there would have been loud wails for him. Here, tears were contained by handkerchiefs dabbing at eyes. At the coffee table, a practice that in itself bemused her, Oge had been shocked to see Gunter's mother and her siblings, whose father they had just buried, smiling, going from table to table asking their guests if they had enough to eat, to drink, as if the guests were the ones needing consolation and not they. They, the recently bereaved, would burst into laughter occasionally at something someone said. *When I die, you'd better tell our children to cry for me the Nigerian way and to send me off the Nigerian way,* she had told Gunter later. *Or I'll come back and haunt them all.* She had only been half joking.

And yet, when Jordi died, she discovered that she could not cry. Instead she watched as Nonkel Gust, Gunter's great-uncle who everyone had thought would die two years earlier when he fell for the second time and broke a hip, gingerly lifted a croissant to his mouth. She watched him wipe off the flakes that stuck to his lips. He said, *What a perfect croissant.* Why was he alive, Oge wondered, and not Jordi? Why were all these people, old enough to be Jordi's parents and grandparents (and great-grandparents even), still alive while her son was gone?

The Belgian pastor, the same one who had only an hour before stood in the pulpit and talked of death not being final where people of faith are concerned, had given her a little encouraging smile. She scowled at him. She wanted them out. All of them. She wanted to shout and scream and ask for Jordi until Death itself heard and released him. She could no longer see through the tears that clouded her eyes but, as if in compensation, her hearing sharpened and all the voices assaulted her. *Such a pity... Poor kid... Lovely sandwiches... Try the chicken spread, it really is delicious... And the eclairs? Some bakers plaster on too much chocolate but this is just right!*

Oge could not bear it any more: these people, friends and family who had gathered to mourn with them, eating and talking with terrible normalcy. And Gunter! Gunter, who ought to hurt as much as she did, was at that moment bringing a sandwich to his mouth in the same relaxed way he did at the breakfast table. Jordi had only been dead four days. Her throat burned. She stood up, almost upending the table she was sitting at, said words she no longer remembered, and stormed out. Gunter ran after her, and managed to catch her by the wrist. *Please, come back inside, darling.* He knelt on one knee as if he were asking her to marry him all over again. She wrenched her wrist from his hand. *You've got breadcrumbs all over your mouth,* she said. *Go back to your people. I hate all of you!*

That evening, she locked Gunter out of the bedroom. He slept on the couch. In the days and weeks that followed, Oge continued to refuse to sleep in the same room as him. She moved into Jordi's room, curling herself into a ball to fit into his bed, screaming into the bedsheets that still smelled of him, trying to shut out Gunter's voice pleading with her, asking her to get help, finding fault with her.

Why don't you get dressed? It's afternoon already. You can't be walking around in your dressing gown.

Oge, wake up. You've been in bed the whole day.

Oge, you shouldn't be drinking alone. It's dangerous.

She hated the ease with which he had thrown himself back into life. Eating and drinking and seeing colleagues after work as if nothing had happened. She could not bear to go back to work. And could he stop with the damn talk about seeing a therapist? She did not need a fucking therapist to tell her how to deal with... with... She was unable to get the words out, but she felt them coalesce and form a fire that threatened to incinerate her. *What does your therapist know about being a mother to a child who goes to school one day and never returns? I'll drink as much as I fucking want to drink.*

One night, they threw accusations at each other, flinging them with careless abandon, and she screamed at him to go, to take his clothes and leave. *Fuck off and never come back! I'm done with you. I hate you! Go! Go!* And he went. He packed a small suitcase and walked out, locking the door behind him.

Oge had wanted to spend the rest of her life in bed, thought that she would, because what was there to do? CM, the health insurance company she worked for, was generous with her time off, and with a doctor's note she could get as much time as she needed. *I think you might find it useful to throw yourself into work*, the doctor said, writing her a prescription for antidepressants. She binned the prescription. No amount of pills would take her pain away. And as for throwing herself into work, she did not know if she would ever be ready to walk back into CM. She had no desire to sit behind a desk sorting out claims. She could not stand the thought of seeing her colleagues, not even Sofie with whom she was friendly, and who had left her many messages asking if she could do anything, if she could help with anything. Oge did not call her back because what was the point? She avoided her friends. She did not want to hear the platitudes. What did any of them know about losing a child? On the day of Jordi's funeral, a woman she knew from church had actually told her, *I know how you feel.*

No, you don't, Oge had snapped, turning her back on the woman.

Sometimes at night, she wished for the comfort of something familiar, her old bed in Enugu, her mother's jollof rice, her father's hand in hers. One morning, she got up, dressed and walked to the travel agency on Gasthuisstraat and bought a ticket to Nigeria before she could change her mind. On the long plane journey from Brussels to Lagos, Oge tried not to think of an earlier visit, when Jordi was one. She and Gunter had taken him to Nigeria to visit her parents, bringing with them his favourite teddy bear at the time, a brown bear in a velvet waistcoat. They flew home without the bear and, in the years that followed, it had been forgotten, long replaced by other favourites.

When Oge walked into her old room, the same room she had shared with Jordi and Gunter that holiday, the bear was on her bed. *I wasn't sure whether to*—her mother began to say, but Oge shook her head to cut her off. This unexpected piece of Jordi was a sign that she had done the right thing coming here. She held the bear to her chest and kissed it as she would a child. And then she began to cry. It was the first time she had cried since Jordi died.

As she walked home from the shop, she decided that, after baking Jordi's birthday cake, she would take his presents and his teddy bear to the cemetery and come back home, turn the heating to the max, and get drunk. She would not think of Gunter, who had not returned her call. She would get through today by herself. But the thought of Gunter slithered in. She missed him. What was it her mother had said, two days ago? *You and Gunter should be doing this together. You both lost a son. Whatever it is he's done, forgive him.* Her mother's parting words at the airport. But what was there to forgive? She was no longer appalled by the fact that Jordi was cremated. *So what if Igbo people do not cremate?* her father had asked. Jordi was hers and Gunter's alone. Her grief was hers and not that of the entire Igbo people. *Do you still love him?* She did.

What if it's already too late? What if he never comes back? she whispered to her father.

Then you go to him, Oge. You ask him to come home.

But why was Gunter so compliant? Why did he not resist? Why did he not put up a fight when she asked him to leave? What if it was because he was fed up with her? Maybe he had already met someone else? Her father calmed her fears. *He left to give you room,* he said. *Faith as small as a mustard seed,* Oge thought.

She called Gunter yesterday as soon as she got in from Zaventem, tired from the overnight flight, and left a message asking him to call her back, please. *We need to talk,* she said. But he had not called back. What if he never did? What if he did only to say he was sorry but he'd moved on? In that case, she told herself, opening the door to the building, she would learn to live without him. Bereft. Hollow. Regrets. If her visit in Enugu had taught her anything, it was that time makes it possible to pick up and carry on. She, who never imagined returning to work, had her clothes ironed and was ready to go back in a few days. By the time she climbed the thirty steps to their front door Oge was worn out. She should have taken the lift but she had always had a fear of enclosed spaces.

Gunter was in the house when she got in, as if her thinking of him had conjured him up. He was in the kitchen, doing the dishes she left behind this morning. She stood and watched him for a moment, and a part of her that was cold began to thaw. She thought of all the ways in which she loved him.

'I hope you don't mind,' he said.

'Don't be silly, it's your house too,' she replied. As if it had not been three months since she kicked him out, since she was with him last, as if it were just another day. Her heart was racing and she tried to still it. She held out the shopping bag and the racing car she was still carrying. 'For Jordi.' She said it for something to say. She knew she did not have to tell him who the presents were for. Jordi, with his voice high and questioning: *Mama, why are you brown? Papa, what does this word mean?*

With that mind, Jordi will surely be a scientist, Gunter said once. Jordi, with that mass of curls inviting you to bury your nose in it.

With that hair, he'll drive every woman crazy, Oge replied.

She held the racing car out to Gunter like a peace offering. 'Here, see? It's remote controlled. Lights blink. Doors open. Everything.'

Becoming Prosperous

'So Yar'Adua goes to Israel on an official trip. He gets sick there and dies. His entourage is told, "Well, you've got two options. Your president was a Muslim and so must be buried quickly. We can bury him here at no cost to you since he was our guest or you can take his corpse home but that would cost a lot. Thousands and thousands of dollars." Yar'Adua's men beg for a few hours to think about it. Five hours later they come back to the Israelis. "Well?" The Israeli president asks. The head of the entourage clears his throat and says, "Your offer is very generous but we'll turn it down. Thing is we all know the story of the famous someone, the son of a carpenter, who was buried here and who rose after three days. We don't want to take that risk!"'

The laughter bursts into the kitchen and Prosperous shakes more salt than she intends to into the simmering pot. It must be John telling jokes again. A raised voice says over the laughter, 'This is an old joke. Yar'Adua's been dead two years already. In any case, you've got it wrong. Muslims are not buried. They are cremated. For their sins, they are burnt. You've not told that story well.'

John shouts the voice down: 'You're the one who is

wrong! Cremation is forbidden in Islam.' A shout breaks out in the room.

Prosperous has had enough. She turns up the volume of the radio beside her so that the music playing fades their voices into the background. It is a cover of Michael Jackson's *Thriller*, in a language she doesn't understand, but soon she is humming along, tapping her feet to the beat, transported to another place. She is startled when she feels a hand travel down her neck. Agu.

'Food almost ready?' he yells above the music.

She yells back, 'Soon.'

He rubs her back, plants a kiss on her forehead and moonwalks theatrically out of the kitchen. In the old days, they would have been doing this together: the cooking and the dancing and the kissing in between. Now, even when she asks, he says he's too tired to help.

In their second year of marriage, Agu had driven over six hundred kilometres from Onitsha (where he had been on business) to Jos, only to find Prosperous in bed with a fever. He had not been too tired then to help her, to nurse her, undressing her and carrying her to the tub to sponge her down. He had not been too tired to fry plantain for her, dismissing the maids because he wanted to look after his wife himself. 'I am not delegating my duty as your husband to someone else,' he had said, encouraging her to eat even though the fever coated her tongue with bitterness and snatched her appetite. When she threw up all over the tiled floor, not making it to the bathroom on time, he had gone outside and scooped sand from their front yard to soak up the vomit. He had cleaned it up and cleaned her up, all the time muttering, 'My poor baby.'

But things have changed and she misses those days, when nothing seemed impossible. What plans they had had when they first arrived. Prosperous laughs when she recounts—as she often does to her friends—the heady expectations of their early days. *I thought they'd take one look at our degrees and offer us jobs on the spot. Company cars, a company house with a massive lawn, a butler and a chef.* Agu never talks of those days. It is as if the weight of remembering is too much for him to bear, but Prosperous doesn't want to forget. Remembering keeps her on her toes.

'If I forget, if I cannot talk about it, I'll think that this is all there has ever been, that I never imagined the possibility of something better,' she told Agu when he scolded her for telling the story to a group of new friends.

She exaggerates of course when she tells the story, mocking their expectations to remove the sting of their reality. *We weren't even offered a pot to piss in!* At one of the job centres, the young man they saw asked them, *Do you speak any Nederlands? Nee? Frans? Nee?* They could not hope to get the kind of jobs they were after, working in a bank or teaching, if they spoke neither Dutch nor French. Ideally, he said, they would need both. Some German and some English would be useful too.

Whenever she retells the story, Prosperous always ends with the same line: 'Haba! All those languages and a teaching degree to be able to teach mathematics to a bunch of kids!'

There are times, mostly at the end of the day, when Prosperous regrets that she did not rise to the challenge. Today, since the phone call with her parents, that thought has not left her head, so that even as she is washing the spinach to go in the egusi soup, she is having a conversation with herself. *Look at Oge! I should have taken language lessons, gone for that teaching degree, refused to settle for this.* She takes the spinach out of the sink and begins to chop. *Instead, we let ourselves be defeated by the thought of going back to school, sitting through lessons to learn not one but at least two new languages. Which is perfectly understandable. No. It's not. In fact, why can't I do it now?* She unwraps two bouillon cubes, drops them in a cup of hot water and begins to stir. *Maybe not the teaching degree but... I could take language lessons at the night school.*

She stops stirring and a small smile begins to spread on her face. The way out has been there all along, why has it taken her hearing about Ifeatu to figure it out? Of course, the language lessons at the Athenaeum. She sees the *reklame* for them all the time. Affordable lessons at convenient hours. Why has it taken this call to make her see that this could be her way out? After all, she knows other success stories: the cousin who moved to Canada in the 90s with nothing but a BA degree in English and no work experience, for one. Now, that cousin is a professor in one of Canada's top universities. Maybe they should have gone to Canada too. Once she said this to Agu and he reminded her that they had had no choice. Belgium had been foisted on them. But her working as a cleaner and Agu at a bread factory was not forced on them, she reminded him. 'Go find me that office job that I refused to take and I'll start today!' he responded angrily. *We shouldn't have given in so easily. We should never have left. We would have been better off in Nigeria.*

And yet they—like many of their friends who visit every weekend—cannot return until they have made enough money, acquired enough material possessions, to be seen as successful. *What would be the point of going back to Nigeria with nothing but the clothes on your back?*

Prosperous cannot remember now who told the story of some relatives who returned from somewhere in Europe after many years abroad with not even a car to their name. 'They could not even afford to build a house! They were booed each time they showed their face at any family gathering, so they stayed away!' Prosperous felt sorry for this couple she did not know but Agu said they should have known better. 'Who goes overseas and returns with just the spittle in their mouth? I'd rather die!'

The men will do anything but clean. 'That's a woman's job,' Agu said once when they saw a vacancy for a cleaner. It would kill him to do that and how could she have thought that he would? 'Abi you want to turn me into a woman?' In Nigeria, Prosperous reminded him, he had cleaned. Before they got maids, they had shared the chores. 'But that was different,' Agu said. 'Remember the pinny game?' he asked, smiling, cupping her buttocks. Prosperous did. On weekends, they cleaned together, naked save a cleaning apron. In their life in Nigeria, where they both earned enough to be independent, there had been no demarcation of chores, no women's jobs or men's. He would not have thought it insulting to be asked to do "a woman's job".

The music has stopped and the radio is playing something else, a quiz show from the sound of it. She turns it down and is confronted once more by the voices of the men arguing. John is insisting that he is right but gets shouted down. 'Why do you want to spoil a good joke?' Agu asks. He has a beautiful voice. No. She corrects herself. He had a beautiful voice. Deep. Like Barry White's. Meant for serenading (and indeed he had done a bit of singing before all this) but, these days, his smooth, deep voice has become gravelly and rough. It is, Prosperous thinks, like sandpaper rubbing against her ears. He always sounds angry even when he is not. When his tenderness slips through, the voice remains angry. But she has suffered too. They have all known better times. He must not forget that. She has suffered as much as he has. Gave up as much as he did.

Why do they have to be so loud? she wonders, not for the first time today. Everything about them feels wrong here. Even the laughter, which is too expansive for the narrow flat; it might crack the walls and seep into the other flats and then what trouble they would have. Neighbours complaining of raucous laughter.

And this talk about Muslims and burials. The joke does not amuse her. It feels inappropriate after what she and Agu have been through, these jokes about death. Have they not seen enough of it?

The kitchen is hot and she wishes there were a window

she could open. She feels like she is being slowly steamed like the moin moin she is cooking on the bigger burner.

The men are laughing at another joke, but she has not been paying attention. She is thinking of Ifeatu and of language lessons and muting the voice in her head telling her that it is too late. *You can't teach an old dog new tricks!* She heaves the bag of powdered yam out of the cupboard under the sink. In the beginning, she was unable to eat it, firm in her belief that the powder was not yam, could not possibly be yam, but was a combination of chemicals not fit for human consumption. She has no recollection of the precise moment she stopped noticing the taste. Or stopped noticing that the bananas lacked the sweet, rich taste of the bananas of her homeland. Or that her clothes are mostly polyester affairs from the Wibra on Gasthuisstraat.

Her life has come to this. Her years of study have come to this. She has a degree in banking and finance from one of Nigeria's finest universities and five years of experience working in a bank in Jos, going to work in power suits and climbing steadily up the corporate ladder. Sometimes, in her dreams, she revisits that life, but once awake she cannot recall it in detail. Her new life has superimposed itself on the old so that any clear memory of the former is impossible. It frustrates her that she cannot even recall with certainty, for instance, the exact colour of her office desk. Was it burgundy or black?

It does no good to think like this, she chides herself, finally gathering enough courage to taste the soup she

oversalted. *Hmm, not bad.* She stirs in the spinach and
lowers the flame of the burner. She lifts the pot of moin
moin off the burner and almost drops it from the heat.
She wipes sweat off her forehead and makes a mental
note to start defrosting the fish stew to go with the moin
moin for those who might prefer it to the meat stew she
has ready. She has also made soup and pounded yam for
those of them who, like John, cannot stand moin moin.
This is her job: to anticipate the needs of Agu and his
friends. How has she allowed her life to boil down to
this: the anticipation of the needs of these men, as if they
were her children?

She remembers a story she and Agu listened to once
on the BBC. A man comes home from work tired and
hungry. He asks his wife for food, but there is none in the
house—there's a famine or something—she has forgotten
the details. Not wanting to see her husband hungry, she
cuts off a breast and feeds it to him. The next day the
same thing happens. And while she's clearing the table,
the husband asks her why her shirt is all bloody. She tells
him what she's done and he says, 'Great! Now we have to
start on the children!' Agu had laughed and said, 'What
a silly tale. Anyway, we do not have any children for me
to eat!'

In that blurry former life, Agu respected her job,
her need to rest after work. She never felt that she was
sacrificing her life for his. Weekends were spent in bed,
talking about colleagues and dreams and whether or
not to go Saturday-night dancing, and should they start
having babies? They had maids. She did not need to do

any cooking or any housework. Now, he invites people over every weekend, and she has to do all the work.

Sometimes, she wonders what Joke would say if she told her that she, Prosperous, who now cleaned for her, had lived a life where she had people waiting on her hand and foot. Sometimes she thought of those maids and felt guilty at how she had taken their hard work for granted. But she shoudn't feel guilty, should she? She treated her maids well. They ate the same meals that she did. She knew people who fed their domestic help gari and soup every day, who denied them meat and milk. So what if on many evenings, she came home, exhausted from work, and asked the two young girls to massage her feet. She was kind to them. She never beat them. She did not keep a special whip for them like their neighbours in Jos did for theirs. She bought them clothes at Christmas. She bought them shoes from boutiques, the same kind of shoes her friends with children bought their own flesh and blood. So what if the girls (how old had they been by the time they left, surely not older than fourteen?) had not been paid. The arrangement with their parents when the cousins were brought to Prosperous's house in Jos was that she would put them through school, lodge them and feed them, and she had. She had nothing to be ashamed of, surely. Twice a year, when they drove back to the east for Christmas and the New Yam Festival in August, they took the girls along so they could visit their families. She gave them money then for their parents, and presents of sacks of rice and loaves of bread for their families back home. Yet, now, she often catches herself

wondering why she could not also have paid them. She
and Agu could have afforded it. It did not matter that
many of their friends did the same thing. That it was
normal. But it wasn't really, was it? It was unfair.

She remembers being outraged when she discovered
that a friend's maid slept on the cold marble floor of her
kitchen, and told her friend off. And yet when they left
Nigeria, she and Agu simply sent the two girls who lived
with them back to their families in Osumenyi without a
thought as to how they would continue their education.
But what could they have done? Brought the girls to
Belgium with them? She treated them kindly, more
kindly than most, so why this nagging? She wonders
now, if they'd finished their education, would they be
better off back home than she was here?

The quiz show is over and the news is on. Here
and there, she picks out a few words of Dutch but not
enough to get a sense of what the journalist is saying.
This frustrates her, especially today. The Prosperous of
Nigeria would be ashamed of her. That other Prosperous
would have mastered the language, made something of
herself. It was a different life. She and Agu were equals.
Here, surrounded by the odour of their losses, he feels
the need to assert himself as a 'man'. Now he orders her
around in a voice that is also new. He tells her he wants
babies. He is getting old. They should have children.
Maybe four. A sensible, even number. 'And where would
we put the babies?' she asks. *In the closet?* Their flat has a
sitting room, one bedroom, one small bathroom and an
even smaller kitchen, like a doll's house. The hallway is

narrow and will not hold a pram. Where would all their children play? Where would they learn to walk and run around?

In their small bedroom, Agu holds her tight and empties himself in her. She does not always want to but she does not resist him because her body needs the comfort. And there are times when they make love and the old Prosperous and the old Agu slip out of their new skins and she imagines that they are back in Jos, and nothing has changed. 'Are you on the pill?' he asks. Each time she says no. The only response he wants to hear. The room is not big enough, the space is too limited, for any other answer. This place has not only shrunk her but has made her a convincing liar. In that way she has changed, too.

She ladles soup into a huge bowl, careful not to be stingy with the gizzards (special discount from Gbolahan, who works in an abattoir) and stockfish (special discount from John, who helps out at the Oriental Shop when he is not working at a factory as an electrician on call). It helps to have friends in useful places, she thinks, dishing out the too-white pounded yam into a wide platter edged in a trellis pattern (bought second-hand from the thrift shop).

When she was in secondary school, her form mistress began the term once by talking to the class about "intentional relationships". 'Learn to keep friends that can be as useful to you as you are to them,' she told the class of thirteen-year-olds. Prosperous thinks of it now, how useful it would be if they were friends with Ali

and Abdul who work at the thrift shop and could keep
choice items aside for her. But even here, where it no
longer matters, where it should not matter, they still keep
away from Ali and Abdul. Nigerians too, but the wrong
religion. 'The Muslims,' Agu would say when asked. 'I
keep away from the Muslims.' As if the Muslims were a
highly contagious disease.

'You can't blame Ali and Abdul for what happened
in Jos,' she tells him, trying to convince him to make
an effort to return their friendship, the hellos thrown at
him, hoping to elicit more than a tart response.

'I can't forget what they did to me.'

Agu used to have a supermarket. On a street full of
supermarkets, it was a testimony to his business acumen
that his supermarket stood out above the rest. He said it
was all down to strategic planning. It wasn't anything he
had picked up while studying for his accounting degree
(although the degree helped); it was just that he knew
how to place his products so that they caught the eye.
The men's deodorants with the chocolate bars so that a
man who came in with his girlfriend for some chocolate
was confronted with the deodorant he might need. At
Eid-al-Fitr he presented his Muslim customers with clear
plastic bags of ram's meat dripping blood, for which
they thanked him effusively. Yet when the riots started,
that did not save him. Did not save his shop. The name
marked him out as Southerner: Agu and Sons (there
were no sons yet but surely those would come?). The
supermarket was razed and he lost everything in one
night. His investment. His will to live. There was no

question of his wife continuing her job at the bank. She was marked too.

They cleared their joint bank account to buy a passage out. No choice. The man who said he could help them out had only one country he could get them into. Belgium. 'They don't even speak English there,' she complained, but for Agu it was enough that it was far away from Nigeria. 'I don't care if they speak cat. I need to get out of here,' he said, eager to seek a new beginning. He has never been one to look back.

She does not want to think of the charred corpses she saw the day after the riot. She does not want to think of the way human bodies sizzled like pork when they burned. She does not want to think of the trouble it took to get them here. Or of the lies they had to tell, the new identities they had to wear. Their passports say they are from Liberia and it occurs to her that, should she die, the authorities would probably contact the Liberian embassy. In all her years here, she has never even met a Liberian!

She lifts the moin moin from the pot and places them in a round dish, a present from one of her employers. A lonely woman who tells her often, 'No one gets my toilets as clean as you do. You are a treasure'. She knows how to scrub toilet bowls until they gleam. She exerts pressure on the brush and wipes the seat so clean that not a spot of dirt is to be found. She lifts the seat and wipes under it where trails of urine tend to hide. Her boss in Nigeria used to say that she was his most dedicated member of staff, nothing escaped her attention. And now, how easily she has transferred that dedication to toilet bowls and wooden floors. How she has adapted to this life she would never have imagined she would live. Cleaning and cooking and never asking for (or anticipating) help.

She puts the food on a tray and carefully carries it out to the sitting room where the men are now playing a game of Whot. The men hardly look up from their game. When she returns with plates and spoons, all four drop their cards as if on cue and Emmanuel says, 'At last. Smells delicious, nwunye anyi.' *Nwunye anyi,* our wife. That is what she has become. "Wife" to whichever guest her husband invites home: cooking, cleaning.

Her parents suggested that they move in with them while they looked for new jobs. 'I am a broken man,' Agu told her. 'I cannot begin to pick up my pieces here.' She would have liked to stay back, to try to find a job in another bank in the east—she had experience after all—but she imagined Agu, a bag of rattling bones unable to become whole again. Was her love for him not enough to start afresh somewhere else with him? Who was to say she could not make a career in the new country? He would just work long enough to regain everything he had lost in the north and then they could move back. It did not have to be permanent. 'Darling, please,' he said. 'I can't stay here. I'd die.' What was love, after all, if not sacrifice? Prosperous thought and agreed to the move. If anyone asked her now if that sacrifice had been worth it, she would say no. That love that had brought her here, where was it now? The Agu for whom she moved to Belgium, where was he now? There were days when she felt as if someone had stuck a knife in her back and any sudden movement might kill her, and so she moved slowly and quietly like a ghost through her own home, building up the courage to pull that knife out once and for all.

Since coming here three years ago, they have stopped talking about their work to each other. Agu working in the bread factory, transferring hot loaves from one machine to the other (at least that is what she thinks he does, she is not entirely sure), not making nearly enough to replace what he has lost. She says nothing about vacuuming floors and wiping windows, in light tones as if it did not matter, as if she found satisfaction in those menial jobs, as she had done at the beginning.

The words they do not say fill the distance they keep from each other, except when there is fault to be found in this new world where roles are demarcated. When the food is not ready on time. When the flat is not tidy enough. Or her voice is not "wifely" enough. Then Agu unleashes his frustrations on her. His hand connects to thump sense into her. And her hands find their way to thump him back. In this way too, they have changed. Afterwards he cries and says he is sorry but when a man works all night in a bread factory it changes him. He feels like his life is careening away from him, he says, and he has to find a way to regain control. 'I am sorry, I am sorry,' he says. She never says anything. She never says she is sorry for hitting back. She never absolves him. When the old Agu returns and he rubs her back and kisses her neck and moonwalks out of the kitchen and holds her

tight while they dance at parties in Antwerp and Brussels
and Bruges, she does not feel the smug satisfaction she
used to of someone in love. Today, especially, she feels
an impatience to begin another journey.

'Our wife!' someone shouts. 'Our wife! Bring us
another glass, please.' Prosperous pretends not to hear
although the flat is so small there is no way she could not
have heard.

The phone call with her parents earlier in the day is
playing on a loop in her head. 'How is work?' her father
asked.

'Fine. Doing well.' Her parents have never asked her
what she does but she knows that they assume that both
she and Agu are doing the sort of jobs where they sit
behind desks.

'I saw Ifeatu,' her father said. Prosperous could hear
the excitement in his voice before he said, 'She's running
for governor of Enugu State! Your friend could be our
governor!'

Prosperous's mother shouted in the background,
'Hasn't she called you yet?'

Suddenly, the phone grew so heavy in Prosperous's
hand that she could no longer hold it up. She was happy
for Ifeatu, her roommate and friend at university, who
had spent many weekends with her family. Ifeatu would
spend the evenings after dinner discussing politics with
Prosperous's parents with a passion that Prosperous
herself did not share. It was not that she was not interested
in politics, but she thought that Ifeatu was too interested.
Back then, Ifeatu used to tell anyone who would listen

that she would become the president of Nigeria one day and she would make Prosperous the Accountant General of the Federation.

'From all indications, her party is going to win!' her father said and the pride in his voice was a dagger in Prosperous's heart.

She is happy for her friend but she knows that if Ifeatu called her now, she would not answer. She would not say that she is jealous but she needs time to get over how far apart their lives have drifted. If Ifeatu could chase her dreams, why can she not? They were both ambitious as undergraduates.

'Prosperous! Another glass, please.' It is Agu this time. Prosperous ignores him. *You can walk to the kitchen and get it yourself! You have legs.*

It's decided. Tomorrow, she will register for Dutch lessons. She does not care how long it takes, she will master this language. I have sacrificed enough! She knows from Joke that the VDAB runs courses at little or no cost for the unemployed. Once Prosperous has enough proficiency in Dutch, she will register for one of those. Maybe a course in graphic design? Develop that artistic side of hers that she has not yet had a chance to explore. Maybe a course in bookkeeping? Something closer to her original degree. Maybe try something completely new, do something radical: study to be a printer. Or a mechanic. Why not? She has always liked cars. How she used to enjoy it when her father let her tinker with his car engine, how much pride she took in being asked, at the age of nine, to help change the car oil. The possibilities are endless.

'Nwunye anyi?' a voice yells from the sitting room.

'Prosperous!' Agu yells at the same time.

'Fuck off!' Prosperous shouts back.

Everyone Deserves Grace

Agu met Prosperous on a Friday night. By Tuesday, he'd called his father and told him he'd found the woman he would marry. He had only been half joking, after all, he didn't know her well enough. But on the Sunday after they met, they had gone out for a meal together. He had felt relaxed around her, as if he had known her since birth. At the end of the evening, when his car wouldn't start, she had asked to take a look at it for him. 'Don't call a mechanic yet, let me.' He had thought that she was joking and had burst out laughing. She asked him to switch on his headlights. He humoured her. The lights came on strong and bright. She opened the bonnet, asked him to get a stone. 'I probably need to dislodge the kick-starter,' she said. When next she asked him to turn the ignition, he did with little expectation—even though he had been impressed that she knew what a kick-starter was—and so the engine revving disarmed him. He sat in the car like one hypnotized even after she'd closed the bonnet. 'Told you!' she said, when she came round to his side of the car, giving him a boastful wink, smiling the easy smile of conquest. He thought he understood now what was meant by being swept off one's feet. She was an undertow, pulling at him. Everything about her, from the fire in her eyes to the mole between her eyebrows thrilled him.

'Thanks, that was... incredible.' She was incredible. Extraordinary. Magical. He couldn't stop the thoughts invading his mind. He couldn't stop thinking how lucky he was to have been introduced to her by a mutual friend. He came out of the car and stood in front of her.

'I'd like to do this again,' she said.

'You'd like to peer into the engine of my car?' he asked and they both laughed. When he leaned in to kiss her on the cheek, she took his face in his hands and kissed him on his lips.

He was thinking of that now as he pushed pallets of bread to the Lidl vans waiting outside. The remembrance made him smile. His nine-hour shift at the bread factory was almost ending. The city was stirring but his night began in the morning. He wanted nothing more at that moment than to go home, sneak into bed and make love to his wife, love her back into the woman she had been in Jos who had told him that his hands were magic. When they made love these days, she lay unpliable underneath him, immune to his hands. It broke his heart each time, and he wished then, that he could love her a little less. If he did not love her, if he still did not find her attractive, if she did not still pull at him, he could have given up on the lovemaking completely. But he could not live with her and not have her. It felt to him, more than ever, that she had already checked out and he was playing catch up. And after yesterday, after what he had done to her, how could he ever, ever hope to bridge the gap?

He had felt like that—playing catch up—when they first started dating. He wouldn't say that he had found her intimidating; he loved her confidence, the way she walked into a room and *owned* it, but it bothered him more than just a little that they came from opposite worlds. The first time they visited her parents in Enugu, and he had seen how she grew up, his old insecurities had come flooding back. He saw Prosperous's old room with its own desk and chair ('I remember going to choose those,' she told him), sat in Prosperous's parents' sitting room with an old colour TV ('They've had that TV since I was a child!') and felt again like the 8-year-old child in Okpoko, Onitsha whose father was too poor to buy a television. No, not that 8-year-old, he corrected himself, because at that age, he had been surrounded by people who lived like him and hadn't realized that they were poor. He remembered days with the other TV-deprived neighbourhood boys his age outside, "driving" by rolling discarded tyres with sticks. Agu remembered his father telling him about his mother, with whom he had been so in love that after she died giving birth to Agu, he never remarried.

'No woman will ever come close to your mother. She was an angel,' he always said, so that Agu imagined his mother dressed in the boubou she wore in the photograph of her on the wall of their living room (which was also where he and his father slept) with huge wings fanning out each side of her.

At 12, Agu had earned a scholarship to CKC, Onitsha, one of the nation's top schools. And it was there that it dawned on him that there were others, young people like himself, who led lives he could never have conjured up. There were the Lagos boys, students whose families lived in the megacity and who always stuck together. The way they walked, the way they talked, the way they spoke about the city evoked reverence in the rest of the students. Those Lagos boys were easy to spot: Obi, Kayode, Kanene in his year. Kayode's father was the pastor of First Baptist Church where US President, Jimmy Carter, visited in March 1978 on his trip to Nigeria, just five months before Agu began his first year at CKC. Kayode had a picture with Carter, which earned him the nickname, Carter Keteke. They talked about horse riding at the bar beach, swimming at Eko Club, watching cricket at Kings College (where Carter Keteke said he'd tried to get into but didn't score high enough for and CKC was the next best thing). Obi's father was someone high in Obasanjo's government and was a member of Lagos Yacht Club. He'd tell anyone willing to listen about sailing on the Yacht with his family to Sea School Island and Tarkwa Bay and having parties in his house where young boys like them drank "33" Export Lager beer. They talked of Fanti carnival and dancing to live bands. It seemed like a different world, not even in the same country that Agu lived in. Agu and his fellow Onitsha boys were mesmerized by those tales. Or perhaps, it was truer to say that he was, because there were *levels* to the local boys. There were people like Enoch, Ndubisi, Eloka and Obidigbo who lived in GRA and for whom Lagos did not hold the allure

it did for him. Eloka's mother was American and for
that, even the Lagos boys respected him. When Carter
Keteke sighed and said 'Ah, Lagos never sleeps! Onitsha
is just too tame!' Eloka shut him up promptly by asking
if Lagos's restlessness could be compared to that of New
York. Carter Keteke might have taken a picture with
Jimmy Carter but Eloka had walked the streets of the
US capital and of New York. But America was too far
away to dream of, too abstract to make sense of, and
so Agu seized on Carter Keteke's words, tailed him and
his mates, took their jabs at his "Onitsha bush ways",
laughed with them when they called him Okoro Feeling
Funky and swore that one day, he too would visit Lagos,
he too would be rich and have adventures worth talking
about. His children would be pampered. What his father
could not give him, he would give his children.

He did live in Lagos for a little while after university
before falling for the temperate climate of Jos and moving
there. And he had loved Jos, loved setting up a business
and doing well until the riots when he lost everything.

As he unlocked his bicycle, ready to go home, his mind
was still on Prosperous and on the life they could have
had, snatched away by hoodlums in Jos and exacerbated
by his uncontrolled temper. The way Prosperous had
looked at him once the boiling water hit her back. He
saw her face transform from shock to confusion and
finally, settle into disappointment. He had said he was
sorry, he had regretted it immediately, but Prosperous
had said nothing in response. If they had never left Jos,
he would never have become this version of himself he

had difficulty recognizing. With his supermarket doing well and plans to expand, he could have given whatever children they had (and he had hoped that they would be many) a luxurious life. Although Prosperous had a well paid job and didn't need his money, he still treated her, bought her things "just because." Belgium had seemed like a good idea, somewhere he could recuperate from his losses and start afresh, but no one had warned him of how low they would have to go. No one had warned him of how it could transform a man. Of how it would steal the fire from Prosperous's eyes. Often, he felt guilty but something (embarrassment?) stopped him from admitting to Prosperous that he wished they had never moved here. Or that even though he prayed for children, he worried too that they would not have the life he had mapped out for them.

When they started dating, he had not wanted to take Prosperous to Onitsha to see his father. The old man had refused to move from the one bedroom flat he lived in even when his son had enough money to move him to a much better house, in a much better part of town. When Prosperous suggested, on their trip to Enugu to visit her parents, that they went to Onitsha too, he made a murmured excuse. He could not tell her that he was too embarrassed to let her see where he grew up, the communal courtyard where people cooked on kerosene stoves, the gutters that curved and stretched along the road which served as toilets and dustbins for inhabitants who had long come to accept their position as the forgotten of the state, the one room he had grown up in, the shared roofless bathroom built of zinc sheets. When his father eventually came to visit them in Jos, he complained about how wasteful they were, how the help sliced off too much of the end of yams *(Haba! What that girl cuts off can feed a grown man!)*; how they had two refrigerators (one in the kitchen and one in their bedroom) when one would do. He rationed water too, not flushing the toilet in the guest bedroom he used after every use. It intrigued Prosperous, this difference between his father's parsimoniousness and Agu's extravagance. She did not understand it, she said. 'You both like extremes!'

Agu's father had been on the brink of wealth before the Biafran war broke out. He and two other friends had a liquor store. 'Business was doing well. We were in talks with a company in Spain to be the sole suppliers of Perry Brandy when the war broke out and put an end to that.' After the war, like every other Biafran, he lost whatever money he had in the bank and was compensated with 20 Nigerian pounds by the victorious government. 'What could anyone do with that amount of money unless you were a magician?' Having lived through the war and having been poor for so long, his father was very cautious around wealth, he told Prosperous. With Agu, having tasted poverty had the reverse effect on him. He was determined to douse himself in his wealth so that none of the stench of poverty remained. And he needed not just the physical things that money could buy but also witnesses to his wealth. It filled him up like food to host friends for lavish meals, to hear them praise the quality of the dishes and the drinks they were served.

Continuing the tradition in Turnhout rooted him to a past he hoped to return to someday. It made his loss bearable. Prosperous had asked him once why they had to have their friends over every week for 'these mini parties,' but he could not tell her. She should be able to see, he thought, that he needed it. That they needed it. 'I spend all day cooking,' she complained. 'You never help!' If she worked nights like he did, standing on his feet, watching out for old, dented bread tins that might clog the oven exit because the factory owners were too cheap to replace the tins, reaching under the moving conveyor belts to pick up bread that might have fallen (they had been warned never to hit the emergency stop button because doing so kept the loaves in the oven longer and they browned too much to be sold and the factory lost money 'and if you lose us money, you won't be paid,'), heaving sacks of flour, pouring buckets of nuts into the right mixer for their "Bread'n' Nuts", pushing pallets of bread, she would know that expecting him to help, that asking him to help, was unreasonable. Besides, she had the other women. They always disappeared into the kitchen with her. 'You swan in and out of the house,' she said once, 'and go straight to bed.' Her words had stung him. Did she really think that what he did was "swanning"?

In a few days, he would be 48. He should be a father to many children now, living in his eight bedroom home in Jos (with a German Shepherd, a swimming pool and a tennis court in the backyard), with a wife who had the same fire in her eyes that had excited him years ago. He shouldn't be riding home on a bicycle so early in the morning, a cap pulled down to cover his ears from the bite of the cold. When she complained at the beginning of having to work as a cleaner, he had been too ashamed to talk of his own job, the continuous, boring drudgery of it. A child might make things better, might fill him up the way having visitors in Jos gush over his wealth had. He was tired, so, so tired. 'Babies bring strength,' his father always said. 'If I didn't have you to look after, I would not have survived your mother's death.'

He could see his building now, illumined by street lights. It was morning but not quite clear yet. He got off his bike and rolled it the rest of the way to the building. At the door, he ran into a neighbour, a man much older than he was but with the energy of a much younger person. It did not matter what type of weather it was, the man was always out at the same time walking his dog. Every time they met, his greetings were always effusive. 'Hallo!' the man said. Agu returned the greeting. He reached down and patted the dog which had jumped up, in its usual fashion, to him for acknowledgment. 'She likes you. Of everyone who lives here, you're the one she likes the most,' the man said to Agu. 'She isn't always this happy to see everyone. Or if she is, she's too proud to show it!'

Agu stood in the cold and watched the man and his dog walk away, thinking of how it was only white people that would characterize a dog as proud. And then he thought of Mr. Iwejuo, his Form 1 Bible Knowledge teacher at CKC who began each class by writing 'pride' on the blackboard in huge, curling letters and drawing a stick figure on the ground behind the word. He called it a "Meditation on Humility." While Agu stood there, thinking of Mr. Iwejuo's lesson, the teacher's voice came to him as clear as if he was standing there with him. 'Pride goeth before a fall.' The teacher had the class chorus this before every class. 'If you do not want to fall, get rid of pride,' he told them. 'But when you fall, as mere mortals do, remember this: all have sinned and everyone deserves grace.' Years after Mr. Iwejuo's "Meditation on Humility" spawned racy jokes amongst mischievous young boys about Grace being a girl from a neighbouring school, the lesson they were supposed to learn unravelled itself to him.

It struck him that it wasn't embarrassment that stopped him from talking to Prosperous about his job, that stopped him from accepting her parents' offer when he needed it, that stopped him from admitting to her that he felt guilty. It was pride. The same pride that made him want to keep up the lifestyle he had in Jos even though Prosperous had to bear the brunt of it. The very same pride that made him (and here, he paused, wanting to cry) raise a hand against Prosperous, pour boiling water on her for shaming him. For telling him to "fuck off" in front of the other men. He was that stick figure on the floor, felled by his arrogance. But would he get grace from Prosperous? If he could not forgive himself, would she be able to? He hoped so, oh he so desperately hoped so. He let himself in, ready to become a new man, deserving of grace.

Better Never
Than Late

The church was unusually cool for an April morning, thanks to the air conditioning. That was one of the reasons why Kambi had transferred. It was one of the few in the city with a working generator and fully functional air conditioning. Unlike others she had tried and discarded like old scarves, *The Holiest of Holies Jehovah Jireh Jehovah El Shaddai Evangelical Church of God* had both air and spirit. She felt it as soon as she stepped in, the first time she visited the church. That first day, the spirit had whirled around her head like a wind and she had heard people in the congregation let forth a slew of words neither she nor anybody else understood. She had lived thirty years without knowing she had it in her: this gift of tongues. But Pastor Moses Elijah Samuel Okeke had helped her discover it. The pastor had come to her and laid his hand on her head and told her, 'Open your mouth and let it out.'

Kambi felt his gold ring pressing on her forehead, felt the cool promise of it all. Her legs began to quiver as he spoke. 'Let it out oh sistah! Release your tongue, sistah! Let the spirit speak through you!' He would not budge until she had shut her eyes, and opened her mouth. Her tongue was tied. 'Focus,' the pastor whispered fiercely into her ears. He said, 'Imagine that the Holy Spirit is a dove perching right now on your shoulder, sistah.' Kambi focused. The darkness in her mind cleared and conjured up two doves perched one on each shoulder. Kambi opened her mouth, and oh, what words had flown out in that single moment. Now she was an expert tongues-speaker.

Kambi was in top form this morning. This was not just an ordinary service. Today had been reserved for exorcism. And not just any exorcism, but that of a witch, and at Kambi's personal request. It was revealed in a dream to her cousin, Ada, who lived with her, that Kambi had remained unmarried after all her fasting and special prayer requests because of Ijeoma.

'That's what you get for doing some of these girls a favour,' she said, as if Kambi had knowingly handpicked a witch to work for her. When she went scouting for a maid, Ada had advised her to get someone from home, someone whose family they knew. Ada knew someone who would be perfect for the job and promised to supervise the girl, but Kambi was all too aware of the sort of trouble that could cause. Ejim, her colleague, never stopped complaining of how her house was overrun by her maid's family and because they were related to Ejim too, she could neither sack the maid nor ask the visitors to leave. No way Kambi was going to make that mistake, so instead of someone from her village, she had asked the security man at work if he knew someone she could employ.

Two days later, he turned up with a small, dark girl who walked with a limp.

'Forget the limp,' he said when Kambi's eyes settled on that unfortunate leg. 'This one here works like a jackie.' And she did. Ijeoma was worth the five thousand naira agents' fees Kambi paid the gateman. And the three thousand she gave the gateman for Ijeoma's family every month. The girl had never given Kambi any reason to complain until two days ago when Ada had her revelatory dream. Kambi was all for kicking her out of the house immediately but Ada, who had been born-again since she was thirteen and was clearly more experienced in spiritual matters, said, 'You need to bind her first so that she can release your luck, then you can kick her out if you want to.' Kambi conceded. It had only been a few years since she'd "seen the light". She had two degrees, but enough self-knowledge to know that she was out of her depth here. Ada spoke with the authority of one who had done this before, telling Kambi of how she had been one of the few prayer warriors in her former church, tasked with helping the pastor when he performed exorcisms. 'To fight these demons, Kambi, your spirit has to be strong like a rock!' And God had blessed Ada, with a strong spirit, in addition to giving her the gift of "sight."

Before becoming born-again, Kambi had never attributed any meaning to dreams. When she was introduced to Freud in Pyschology 101 in her first year of university, she argued with her classmates that Freud was wrong. Dreams did not represent anything, they were just random images, she said. 'But they are not,' the Pastor who baptised her years after she left university and became religious told her. Dreams were messages from God but not everyone had the gift of interpreting them. Only those with the gift of "sight" knew how to untangle their dreams to find the message in them.

The way it was shown to Ada, Ijeoma was a witch and had tied up Kambi's luck since entering her house. Now that Kambi thought of it, it explained a lot of things. She was not ugly. She had, in fact, been a runner up in the Miss Campus Beauty Contest at university. She had a good job working in the Human Resources department of an airline. In the past year alone, she had fasted and prayed more times than she cared to count, to meet a suitable man. In the past two years, she had not even had a serious relationship. It was not that she was afraid of being alone, or "dying alone" like one of her aunts dramatically put it. She just wanted those aunts (and uncles) and her mother to stop asking her, 'Kambi, when are we meeting the one?' whenever she turned up to family gatherings alone, asking in tones that insinuated that it was a shortcoming of hers that prevented her from getting married. There was nothing wrong with her, so why could she not find a husband?

'Your husband is being held from you by that witch,' Ada assured her. 'She has powerful spirits working through her. Do you know how she got that limp?'

Kambi said it was from a polio infection she had had as a child. That was what the security guard had told her.

'Nonsense!' Ada laughed. 'She sacrificed that leg for

her powers. I saw it in a vision. Powerful spirits in her! And you know what else? You remember when Agu visited with his wife before travelling? Ijeoma tied up Prosperous's luck too.'

Kambi would have laughed had anyone but Ada, her serious, pious cousin said this. Before being born again and discovering that evil spirits roamed the world, she would have laughed this off, even if it had come from Ada, but now it made sense. No wonder her cousin and his wife were yet to be blessed with children. She suddenly remembered that Ijeoma had flitted around the couple, asking every second, 'You want something anty? You want something onkul?' And they had thought that she was just being thoughtfully solicitous. Agu had even said, 'What a gem of a maid you have here, Kambi. Small but mighty!' And all the while the witch was busy plotting evil against them. Agu wanted babies. He said so himself every time they spoke on the phone. He could not understand why his wife was unable to conceive. Now, they knew the source of his childlessness. 'What a wicked child,' Kambi said. 'What do we do now?'

'We will beat out a confession from her and get the pastor to bind her on Sunday. We will fight her spirits!'

The beating was necessary, Ada explained, because it meant that once Ijeoma confessed she would be powerless to harm Kambi for a while. 'And before she can regain her strength, the pastor would have bound her and thrown away the key!' Ada shouted triumphantly. But to be on the safe side, Kambi was not to eat any food Ijeoma made. Ada took over the shopping and the cooking. Jobless, a year after graduating from university, she had the time for these things. It was the least she could do for the cousin who had taken her in and offered her a roof, she told Kambi, waving away her gratitude.

That Friday, Kambi took the day off. Beating out a confession was a serious chore on its own without the distractions of earthly labour. She had strengthened herself with prayers, led by Ada who had asked angels to be by their side as they took on the witch. Kambi felt full of the Holy Spirit, as if it were food she had eaten until she could eat no more. She was ready. Ada had told her to catch the little girl unawares. 'Do not give her time to make up stories and confuse you.' Ijeoma was dusting the centre table when Kambi came to her from behind. *Thwack!* The first lash of the koboko landed decisively on her back. 'Anty?' She turned to look at Kambi, her eyes wide, like someone who had seen something scary, a ghost maybe.

'Witch! You think I don't know, eh?' The koboko whizzed through the air and landed on Ijeoma's back. *Thwack!*

'Anty?' She writhed.

Thwack! It landed close to her face.

Ijeoma slid to the floor, hunched her back and buried her face in her chest to protect it.

Ada, who had been fortifying herself with prayers and a passage from the "Search the Scriptures" pamphlet in her room, came out with a leather belt, screaming 'Confess! Confess! Confess witch!' She began to speak in tongues, interrupting it only with shouts of 'Confess!

Confess!' while she lashed out at Ijeoma with the belt.
'You witch! Confess! Raba dabba Confess!' Kambi had
heard Ada speak in tongues many times, but today, there
was a forcefulness to the tongues that made Ada almost
unrecognizable. It was as if she was in a trance. She
looked like Pastor Okeke did whenever he heard God's
voice. Nothing could break the trance until God finished
speaking.

'I haven't done anything oooo! Mama m ooo! Anwukwa
m ooo!'

Thwack! Kambi landed her another lash across her
breasts. She continued to speak in tongues.

'I'm not a witch ooo!'

Thwack!

'Anty, you'll kill me oo.'

'Confess!' *Thwack!* One across the head from Ada.
'Rabbi shaddai graam graam.'

'Anwukwa m oooo! What have I done?'

Thwack! 'You can deny it all you want but I know!'
Kambi shouted.

Ada had warned her that Ijeoma would deny everything.
'She will swear that she knows nothing about witchcraft
but believe me, by the time we're through with her, she'll
tell us the truth, eziokwu. That's how witches are when
they are caught. They'll deny, deny.'

'What have I done?'

Thwack!

'Anty, is this because I didn't give you the change when
I came back from shopping the other day?'

Kambi looked at Ada. Surely, her cousin knew that

Ijeoma was to hand over every bit of change to her, Kambi. She was Ijeoma's boss, not Ada. Why would she ask Ijeoma for the money?

Ada cried, 'The witch is trying to frame me! Which change? Which money? Ramesh ramidiii Jehovah Jire dada gram gram. Confess!' *Thwack!*

The buckle of Ada's belt must have cut Ijeoma because she started bleeding under one eye. Kambi thought maybe they had gone too far. Ijeoma was a child after all. She said, 'Ada, ozugo. Stop.' But Ada, lost in her trance did not hear her. She lifted her head again at the same time as Ijeoma touched the blood under her eye, looked at it and started screaming, 'Yes, Yes. I'm a witch please stop hitting me. Yes! I am. I am sorry. Please, stop!'

Kambi could not believe it. What had she not done for Ijeoma? This girl who had come into her house with one pair of underwear, no bra (even though her breasts had begun to sprout) and two dresses. In the two years she had been with Kambi, her wardrobe had increased, with Kambi's old scarves and hand-me-downs. She even had three pairs of shoes. Leather shoes, not those colourful plastic shoes many maids wore. Kambi, thinking of the fifteen-year-old's future, had wanted her to learn a trade, something that would equip her for life later. She had even started making enquires with Obioma the tailor on how Ijeoma could be apprenticed to him. All that and yet Ijeoma had been fighting her on a spiritual level, slipping witchcraft into the food she served her mistress, whispering spells over her as she slept.

'What have I ever done to deserve that?' Kambi had asked Ada the night before.

'Nothing,' Ada assured her. 'She is eating up your luck to empower herself. You have done nothing!'

The two women sat Ijeoma down in the middle of the sitting room, her back against the centre table.

'How long have you been a witch?' Kambi could no longer shout. A tiredness had settled on her, seeping into every part of her, locking her jaws so that speaking was an effort.

'Eh?' Ijeoma sounded confused. Snot ran down her nose. She wiped it off with the back of a palm. She looked at Ada as if appealing to her to say something but Ada raised the leather belt above her head. Before she could bring it down, Ijeoma shouted, 'A long time!'

'When do you go for meetings with your fellow witches?' Ada asked, picking up the Bible which always lay on the centre table and waving it in Ijeoma's face. There was a wild fire in her eyes. Her voice was loud as if the person she was talking to was in another room.

'Eh?'

'Eh what? Am I talking with water in my mouth? Don't pretend you don't know what I am talking about, or I'll bring out the belt again.'

'At night. I fly out of my body. I fly high-high. Please, don't hit me again. Please, let me go back to my mother.'

Ada looked at her cousin triumphantly. 'See? See? See? Ekwuro m ya ekwu? Did I not tell you? Where is your coven? Is it that mango tree behind Obioma's house?' She held the belt over Ijeoma's head, dangling it like a tail growing out of her hand.

'Yes. yes,' Ijeoma said, trying to stem the bleeding

with a palm. 'I want to go home. Biko nu. Let me go home. Ka m naa uno. Ehhhhh! Ehhh!' She was crying hysterically now, drawing out the ehhhh of her cries.

'Shut up, you amosu! You want to go where?' Ada shouted. 'I told you, Kambi. I told you. She wants to go home so that she can recover her power and finish you off. Go and call the pastor. Now. Call him kita kita, this minute. No wasting time!'

Kambi's hands shook so much as she dialled that her mobile phone slipped out of her hand. She had never seen a witch, let alone lived with one in a house. She had trusted this girl and Ijeoma had spat on that trust. When the pastor answered he said it was a good thing she called as he was about to call her. He had answered at the first ring because he had his phone in his hand ready to call her. Ada had told him all about it. It had already been revealed to him that a member of his congregation had a witch in her house, and that her life was in danger. Ada's call had confirmed it.

'Praise God that you've got it under control now,' the pastor said, 'and that you have a strong sister like Ada to pray for you. On Sunday, we shall bind the spirit of witchcraft in your maid forever.' Kambi got a list of what to bring: a piece of white cloth, a small sack of salt and a bottle of olive oil. Ada offered to do the shopping. She knew where to get everything, and she knew the quality required. 'With things of the Lord, one must not be stingy,' she told Kambi as she pocketed the bundle of notes Kambi handed over to her, picking up some that had fallen from Kambi's shaking hands. Ada held her

cousin's hands until they stopped trembling. 'You'll be
fine,' she said to Kambi. 'The pastor will get the spirit
out of her.'

'Sistas and Brodas! Today we have a very special request!'
Pastor Moses Elijah Samuel Okeke's voice boomed
through and the speaking in tongues and clapping and
dancing stopped. Ijeoma was dragged out by two assistant
pastors, from the Inner Sanctuary where the demon-
possessed were kept until they were cleansed. She wore
nothing but the white cloth Ada had bought, tied under
her arms and reaching down to her knees. Her hair was
mala shaven, so clean the lights bounced off it. Maybe it
was the shaven head, but she looked smaller. There was
a welt where Ada's belt had cut under her eye. Kambi
caught herself feeling sorry for Ijeoma. What if there had
been a mistake? The girl looked harmless. She turned to
Ada and before she had even said a word, Ada said, 'See
how her wild eyes are. Ask the blood of Jesus to cover you
from her evil.' Ijeoma's eyes were indeed wild, Kambi
saw now. They darted over the hushed congregation.
When they landed on Kambi, Kambi shut her eyes and
said a prayer, asking Jesus to cover her with His blood, to
ward off any evil the girl might still be capable of.
    'Brodas and Sistas! This here is a witch!'
    The congregation gasped as if they were being shown
some exotic creature, even though this scene was not
new to many of them, certainly not the older members
of the church. Before Kambi joined, Ada had told her,
the pastor had done at least three exorcisms. One was of

a widowed woman whom her brother-in-law had caught walking around the house at night, mewing like a cat. The pastor had revealed that she was responsible for her husband's death. The cirrhosis of the liver was just a symptom of the woman's sorcery. Like Ijeoma, she had denied it, but confessed during the exorcism. The second one had been of a teenage boy with the spirit of shoplifting. His family was wealthy but no matter how much they gave him, he would still be caught stealing from supermarkets in their neighbourhood. After the exorcism, his parents had bought the pastor a brand new car. The third was a three-year-old whose father's business began to fail the moment he was born and whose mother's womb could not hold a baby after him. Kambi, disturbed by the thought of a toddler being accused of sorcery, asked Ada if the man's business picked up after his son's exorcism. Ada said that if it did not, it was because his faith in the pastor was not strong enough. Kambi might be book-smart, Ada said, but in matters of faith, she was obviously still a learner. 'Today, we are going to cast the spirit in her and send it back to the pits of hell! We are going to reclaim this girl's life for the one true and ever-living Father in heaven. Let me hear Hallelujah!'

'Hallelujah! Amen!' Kambi imagined Ijeoma after the exorcism, freed from witchcraft. She might take her back. She would send her to school, help her live a normal life. She could not help the sense of pride that came over her. She was saving a life! Reclaiming a life for God.

'Hallelujah?' The pastor's voice boomed.
'Hallelujah!'

There was a sporadic outbreak of speaking in tongues.
The pastor raised one hand, the gold ring on his finger
gleaming like the life Kambi imagined would soon be
hers, and a hush fell over the congregation again. He
closed his eyes, mumbled a prayer and slowly started to
sing, his voice deep and sonorous.

My hands are blessed
My hands are blessed
Blessings from the Father, Son and Spirit
Anyone I touch gets their blessing
*Any illness in them I cast out in the name of the Father, Son
and Spirit*

And as he sang, he walked up and down the podium.
He started the song a second time, dragging the words
out as he made his way to Ijeoma. Two men held her,
one at each side, keeping her arms outstretched as if for
a crucifixion.

My hands are blessed
My hands are blessed

He rubbed her bald head as if her were rubbing Aladdin's
magic lamp to release the genie trapped in it.

Anyone I touch...

He touched her face, traced her lips with a finger.

...gets their blessing

He trailed a hand down her throat.

Any illness in them...

He touched her chest and ran his palm down her front. Each time he touched her, Ijeoma jerked and tried to free her hands from the men holding her, but she was powerless against their strength. Done with singing and the blessing, the pastor said, 'Sister Kambi, come forth with the salt and olive oil.' Ada nudged her, Kambi whispered a prayer and, with all eyes on her, walked to the front, clutching the paper bag of salt and bottle olive oil a little tighter than normal. She could feel Ada's encouraging smile urging her on but something stayed her feet.

The pastor took the bag of salt from her, tore it open and poured some on Ijeoma's head. Then he took a pinch and forced it into the girl's mouth. Ijeoma pulled a face and when it looked like she might spit it out, the pastor gripped her by the chin and threw her head back until he was satisfied she had swallowed it.

He faced the congregation. 'This sister might be young,' he said, 'but the spirit in her is as massive as this house, brethren!' There were pockets of nervous laughter as if he had told a good joke. He rubbed olive oil onto his palms and massaged Ijeoma's head so that it shone with an unearthly luminescence.

'Bind her Father shabba rabba Jehovah Niissi.'

'Amen!' the congregation thundered as one.

'Bind her father! Grabba ramidishi wey Jehovah M'kadseh! Take this spirit from her and send it down to the bottomless pit to burn forever and ever.'

'Amen!'

'Let it burn until there is nothing left Father Almighty!'

'Amen!

'Ah! Ranisha dab ah Jehovah rabba ooooo Father free thy servant! Make her thine! Subdue this spirit within her.'

'Amen.'

'Subdue it, tear it out, throw it down into the deepest, hottest part of hell.'

'Amen!'

The pastor shook, from his hand holding the microphone to his legs in their silk trousers. Every part of him trembled.

'Send down your angels, Father. I need strength! Send me an army of angels oh Lord. I am but thy humble servant. Send me an army of angels Father! Jehovah Jire! Jehovah Shammah! Jehovah Rapha! Heal her!'

'Amen!'

'Heal her!'

'Amen!'

'Angels Father! Heavenly armour!'

'Amen!'

Kambi pounded her fists and prayed along with the pastor. She tried to match Ada, praying beside her, in fervour. She closed her eyes and imagined all the angels fighting this battle alongside her pastor; angels in white dresses, flapping feathery wings like huge birds, flying above the pastor to fortify him.

'She's stubborn Father! Make her worthy to wear white like your angels! Shabba dai rabba hallelujah Addonai! Addonai!' He walked off to the side of the podium, reached down and picked up a koboko.

'That's his special exorcism whip.' Ada whispered to Kambi. 'It's authentic cowhide.' He brought it down on Ijeoma with a crack. Kambi flinched. Ijeoma let out a cry, drowned by the stamping of feet and the praying around her but Kambi heard that cry as if Ijeoma were a bird perched on her shoulder. Ijeoma twisted, but could not free herself. When the pastor brought the koboko down again across Ijeoma's calves, Kambi felt as if she herself were being flogged. She could no longer bear to look as the pastor flogged Ijeoma without pausing. On her bare feet. Her skinny ankles. Each time the whip connected with her body, she hopped as if she was treading on hot coals. He flogged her frantically, his arm rising and falling so quickly that the koboko blurred.

The praying and the clapping and the stamping continued. Kambi stood in place, her arms crossed across her chest as if protecting something precious, ignoring Ada's nudges that she clap too. The pastor flogged Ijeoma until the evil spirit in her was defeated and the weight of the exorcism bowed her head and shut her eyes and she no longer resisted. It was only then that the assistant pastors let go of her and she fell like a heap of laundry at the pastor's feet, the white cloth bunched up to expose her thighs.

Then a song of thanksgiving began.

Deep in her heart, where relief should have been a river flowing, Kambi discovered instead that a heartburn had lodged itself, holding her around her neck, so that when she opened her mouth to sing, she could only whisper, 'I'm sorry. I'm so sorry!'

Cunny Man Die, Cunny Man Bury Am

'A man's gotta do what a man's gotta do,' Godwin shouted into Agu and Prosperous's sitting room one January evening. Godwin was small, new in town, and struggling. Prosperous did not know his story. Not entirely. But she could tell that he was a hustler. He had the recognisable tired look in his eyes, the high-pitched tone when he spoke, as if he wanted to convince everyone of his optimism, his certainty that he would achieve whatever it was he had come to Europe for. A man's gotta do what a man's gotta do!

And what a man had to do apparently was marry a Belgian woman. Four months later, Godwin came to visit with his fiancée. Tine was round and soft. She was the colour of dough. She looked like she had the consistency of dough too, like she would dent wherever you touched her, pockmarked by curious fingers pressing her skin.

'She took time finding,' Agu told Prosperous later. Certainly longer than Godwin had anticipated. 'He thought it would be easy. He thought white women were lining up waiting for ndi oji to fall for and marry.'

'That's what they hear back home,' Prosperous said.

'Oyibo women want black men. I remember years ago, our neighbours' son came back from America with tales of how he had to fight off white women. He said that every time he went out, he had to fend off the legion of oyibo women wanting a piece of his black ass. We all believed him.' She laughed at the memory, Agu laughing along.

'Yes, the irresistibility of the black man. Another myth about this place,' Agu said through his laughter. Folded into the edges of his voice, even as he laughed, was the familiar bitterness that Prosperous had learnt to ignore. After all, Agu was not the only one who had to live with failed dreams.

'This is Tine!' Godwin shouted into the room when Prosperous let them in. His smile was too wide, his small frame dwarfed by the woman beside him. His tired eyes gleamed as if they had been polished. Tine smiled a nervous smile and said, 'Hello!' She began to hold out a hand but she also leaned forward as if to offer a cheek, unsure whether to give the traditional three kisses on the cheek or shake hands. In the end she did neither. Godwin held her around her waist and even when they sat down would not let go of her hand. It was as if he were afraid of her slipping away.

'Love nwanti nti,' Agu teased. 'No wound me with your love ooo!'

Godwin snorted and said in Igbo, 'Nwoke ma-ife o na-eme.' A man's gotta do what a man's gotta do.

Tine had large wooden earrings. The sort of earrings that would be described as African because they did not fit anywhere else and Africa was the continent of woods, was it not?

That night, after Tine and Godwin had left and Prosperous was lying beside Agu in bed, he said, '*Ah, that Godwin woman* na room and parlour sha,' as if the thought of Tine's corpulence had just occurred to him. 'Not his usual type but Godwin knows what he's after.'

Prosperous said, 'And so what if she is fat?' She thought Tine seemed too eager to please, too eager to belong. She insisted on eating the poundo with her fingers even though Prosperous had offered her cutlery.

'No, it's fine,' Tine said. 'I've eaten poundo before. Godwin showed me how.' Her earrings jiggled as she spoke. Prosperous could not tell which animal shape they represented.

'Ah, Tine is African woman oo!' Godwin said. 'She's my African queen! She eats fufu well-well.'

He turned her face to his and kissed her on the lips.

'*Love nwanti nti,*' Agu said again and laughed. 'Love in To-Ki-yo!' He broke into 2face Idibia's *African Queen*. Godwin joined him. Then they high-fived each other like teenage boys and started laughing again.

Tine rolled the poundo expertly and, if Prosperous had not been observing her, she would not have noticed that Tine's nose ran from the pepper in the egusi soup, even as she denied that the food was too hot. 'No, no, it's not *pikant*. I like it,' she said each time Prosperous asked solicitously if she would not have preferred something milder.

Prosperous had to fight the urge to tell her, 'No need to

impress this man. He's the one who's too scared to lose you.' She could say it in Flemish, practise her growing vocabulary on this woman. Never having taken Dutch lessons, Agu's Flemish was less than rudimentary. She did not believe that Godwin spoke any at all. They would not understand her. Instead, she said 'lovely earrings' when Tine caught her staring.

'Thanks. Godwin bought them for me.' Her voice had the choked tone of a throat burning with pepper. She stoically struggled on, stopping only to sip some water when her plate was empty.

'But what wasted stoicism,' Prosperous said to Agu, plumping her pillow.

'The girl is happy. Godwin is happy. Why is it wasted?' This Agu who accepted that relationships were a means to an end, who played a part in Godwin's game (but she did too, did she not?), who could not, even now they were alone, condemn his friend, she could not stand.

She reached above her head to switch off the light, plunging the room into darkness.

How could Tine have missed it all? The laughter that was too loud, the waist holding that was too tight? She had control. She, not he. Oh, how Prosperous had wished, several times during the day, that she could shake her, tell her, 'He needs you. Do you need him?' And how could Agu stand it?

She asked him, eventually. 'How can you just sit there and watch your friend use a human being like that?'

'What was he supposed to do?' he asked. Godwin wasn't the only one who married for papers. 'He's not the first and he won't be the last. Besides, he isn't such a bad catch. He treats Tine well.'

A few months later, with flowers in her short boyish hair and a red flowing dress, Tine married Godwin. Agu, Prosperous and several of their friends represented. Tine danced and danced, the dress flowing around her hips like waves. In a corner, her parents sat smiling tightly, clearly intimidated by the too-loud music and the too-wild dancing and the conversations in a language they did not understand, surrounded by a sparse gathering of white, middle-aged couples with identical tight smiles on their faces. 'Watching the natives perform,' Oge whispered to Prosperous, jutting her chin at the white group, shaking her buttocks theatrically to the music.

'My family,' Tine had introduced them earlier. 'They do not understand a Nigerian wedding,' she told Prosperous. 'But I wanted this. I said to Godwin, "You must give me a Nigerian wedding. A Big Fat Nigerian wedding!"' She spread her arms to show how big.

Godwin had a gold stud in his left ear. 'You look like a Hollywood star today-o,' Agu told him.

'I feel like a Hollywood star today! I can float,' he replied as though it was this wedding, this union with Tine, that made him feel like that. But then he grumbled about how much the wedding had set him back, complaining, 'I thought white women were all for equality. That they like to pay their way too. I paid for everything. Even her clothes. Tine did not contribute shi shi.'

'It's all investment,' Agu reminded him. 'You've got to put something in to get something out.'

Prosperous hated this Agu for whom everything, even relationships, was transactional. In all the ways this place had changed him, this was the worst, she thought. Later that night, when they got home, she asked him, 'Must everything boil down to money? It's disgusting.'

'Not to money. To survival. But money is part of survival too, isn't it?' She said nothing and turned her back to him.

At the wedding, Prosperous avoided Tine's eyes, afraid of what the girl might read in them. When she went to say goodbye at the end of the party, she did not say any of the things people said at weddings. Instead she said, 'See you around.' She regretted coming. There was a certain complicity, she felt now, in pretending that this was a normal wedding. It shamed her to be part of it, to have enjoyed it, dancing and eating and chatting. She should have stayed home but all her friends were going, and not just out of solidarity for their Nigerian brother. They all enjoyed a good party.

She could not stand the late nights, Tine said to Prosperous a couple of weeks later. 'He goes out a lot at night. Every night, unless I ask him not to. I wish he'd stay home without me having to say anything. I wish he'd choose to stay home for me.'

Prosperous began to say something, checked herself and stopped. If she were Tine, she would want to know the truth about her husband and she would hope that the woman who called her "sister" sometimes would tell her. But she could not hurt Tine. She said, 'It's a Naija thing.' She hated Godwin for forcing her into complicity.

'He should want to go out together, no? To do things together as a... a... *koppel*, no?'

'Well, you married a Nigerian man. They need to do a lot of things alone.' She hoped the bitterness that coated her tongue did not escape.

'He never takes me anywhere unless I ask!'

Prosperous wanted to take this woman in her arms and knead her, knead her the way she did chin chin dough, stretching it out on the kitchen counter and flattening it out, making it porous enough to let in light. She tried not to think of Tine with flowers in her hair dancing at her wedding two weeks ago. Beautiful, radiant Tine.

'Do you not go out sometimes with Ah-gu?'

'Agu has no time to go out. And neither do I.' This time, she did not have to lie.

'So what do you do together?'

This was something Prosperous could never understand. These people—oyibo people—asked lots of questions. They were never satisfied with subtle answers. They demanded precise, direct responses. Everything had to be measured and set out correctly. If they asked your age, you could not get away with saying you were in your thirties. They wanted to know how old exactly. The system of age grade, where one was not a particular age but belonged to an age group, would never work here.

Prosperous sighed. 'When we are together, we talk. We watch TV.'

'But always inside? You do not go out for dinner?'

'No. No. We do not go out for dinner. Whatever we want to eat, we make at home.' The thought of either

of them suggesting a dinner date was almost laughable.
Every penny had to be counted and preserved. Back
home in Nigeria, they had gone out a few times a month
to a fancy Chinese place where they ordered the same
dependable dish each time: fried rice with sweet and
sour chicken. But here, going out was a frivolity they
could not afford. And besides they had become other
people. Living here and surviving here and waking up
every single day to go to a job neither of them liked had
changed them. She was starting to accept that there was
nothing left of their marriage to salvage. Yet she could
not leave.

'All the time?' Tine asked Prosperous. 'You eat at
home every day?' She sounded like she did not believe
Prosperous. In the heat of the small kitchen, her cheeks
had gone the red of the plastic apples Prosperous kept
in a bowl on top of the fridge to brighten the space,
although she did not think they brightened it up at all.
Tine's forehead was beaded in sweat. She had insisted
on helping Prosperous cook. 'I want to learn his food,'
she said, as if every Igbo dish Prosperous made was
specifically for Godwin.

'All the time.'

Tine came every other weekend for cooking lessons
with Prosperous. She was a keen learner and Prosperous
began to grow fond of the girl. She defended her size
when anyone mentioned it. 'The girl is healthy,' she'd
say. 'She's not chewing-stick thin like all those models
on TV with not a single ounce of fat on their bodies.' Or
she said, 'It's all baby fat. How old is she? Twenty-two?

She's a child. She's young. She'll lose all that fat once she gets older!'

And when Godwin said one thing in Igbo and translated something else when Tine asked, Prosperous called him onuku to his face. Fool. She hissed at him in Igbo, 'You don't deserve her.'

How she wished Tine would see through him and scupper his plans for a shortcut to permanent residence. Let him apply for asylum and be rejected. She imagined that somewhere a guide for beating the system existed for people like Godwin: Marry a Belgian. Follow an integration course for a few days a week. Get your papers in order. Ride it out a few years. Divorce. Then go back home and pick a proper spouse. Everybody knew the deal but the victims themselves. In five years' time Godwin would have Belgian citizenship. He would carry that red passport, be able to get in and get out. Travel to America even, if he chose. That passport was the Holy Grail. The key to free and easy passage through the world.

'Tine shines more and more with every passing day,' Prosperous told Agu one night. Even though Tine kept up her litany of complaints and questions, her skin looked more and more lustrous every time Prosperous saw her, and shone with a brightness that only the truly happy could have.

She said, 'Godwin speaks Igbo all the time so I don't know what he's talking about,' but her eyes glittered like stars. And when she told of Godwin's cousin visiting and spending so much time with Godwin that she, his wife, hardly saw him at all, her lips were stretched into a smile. 'They stay up all night talking,' she said. 'And all day when Godwin is home, they talk too, Godwin and this cousin. I wonder what they talk about? What do they talk about that never finishes? She follows him around like a shadow. When I ask, he tells me it's nothing. Nothing, darling. I just haven't seen her in years, darling, and she'll be gone soon. Then he sits with me. He only spends time with me to keep me from being upset. But I can tell that all the while, he's itching to go back to his cousin.'

Prosperous thought, *Can't she see that this cousin is no relative but most likely a girlfriend, waiting in the wings for the marriage to run its useful course so that she can move in properly?* She felt the anger that should have been Tine's settle on her and she sliced the yam with which she was making pottage with ferocity.

Prosperous wished—as she always did—that she could tell her the truth. But she could not bear to break the heart of this woman who glowed in her marriage. She liked her too much and sometimes imagined that Tine was her own younger sister. What could she say? Godwin is taking you for a ride. He doesn't really love you. He's using you. He's just with you for his papers. And then it would be her word against his. Any idiot could see how besotted Tine was with Godwin.

One day, Tine arrived looking like she had been dipped in oil from head to toe, that was how lustrous her skin had become. Her dark-brown hair shone. Her green dress stopped at the knee and her arms spilled out luxuriously from the short sleeves. She wore silver sandals even though it was gone October and the days had become colder.

'Don't you feel the cold?' Prosperous asked, showing her how to wash beans for akara.

'No,' she shook her head, sending her curls flying. 'I never feel cold. Besides I just had a pedicure done. I must show off my painted nails. *Mooi*, no?'

'Beautiful,' Prosperous said. Lucky for some. She had not had a professional manicure since moving to Belgium. Another extravagance she had given up. In Jos, she had had her nails and toes done every fortnight by Tinuke, the skinny, talkative girl who ran a mobile beauty service.

Tine's dangling gold earrings caught the light of the fluorescent bulb and sparkled. 'You like my earrings? They are presents from Godwin. They are *mooi*, no?'

'Yes. They are very beautiful.' Prosperous passed her a second bowl of beans soaking in warm water. It's a very difficult thing to do, getting all the skin off, she had warned Tine. 'Akara is easy to make but its preparation is hell. It takes a while to get the hang of it, so if it's too difficult for you, don't worry about it.'

Tine dipped her hands in the warm water with the beans and followed Prosperous's lead, her fingers like pink sausages, rubbing the beans against each other with a quiet rhythmic determination, her arms touching Prosperous's. 'Nothing is ever too difficult for me,' she said, not breaking the rhythm of her washing. Her voice was like a knife slicing into the kitchen. It sent shivers up Prosperous arms.

That voice was a stranger's voice and Prosperous had no idea what it meant. She had always been afraid of the unknown. She moved one step away from Tine so that their arms no longer touched.

'Prosperous?' Tine said the name like a question. 'Prosperous?' She kept up the washing, not even raising her head.

'Yes?'

'I know what you think of me. I know.'

'Wha—'

'I know what you think. All of you. John. Oh-geh. Ah-guh. Godwin. Añuli. All of you. I know... I know that you maybe want to protect me so when I ask you things you do not tell me the truth.'

'What are—'

'No. Please. Let me finish.' She lifted a hand out of the water and held up a palm to signal to Prosperous to stop. Water trickled between her fingers like tears. 'You're my friend, my sister, Prosperous, so I'll tell you this. I'll tell you because I don't want you to pity me.'

'I don't—'

'You know you do.' She smiled at Prosperous, a flashing of teeth that was over almost as soon as it began as if she had not meant to smile. 'The day I met Godwin, I thought, What a handsome man! I fell for him. When he said he loved me, I believed him.' She took a deep breath.

Prosperous started to stutter something. Tine cut in. 'It took time, but I know he never did. He... uses me. It hurts but, you see, I loved him. When he asked me to marry him, I did it for myself. Myself. I wanted him. And Prosperous?'

'Yes?'

'He's good in bed. The best!' She paused but Prosperous did not try to fill the silence this time. Tine continued, 'Arm candy to parade around, a man too afraid to displease me!' She let out a chuckle. 'You see,' she put her hand back in the water and continued to wash the beans, 'I said to myself, if he can't love you back, don't let him get away with it, get a big party out of it. I know, I know what you are thinking, but a wedding!' She waved her hands wildly and dipped them back into the bowl. 'I wanted a wedding. Ever since I was little. And I got my dream. I got him to spend a lot of money! Call me petty...' She looked up and held Prosperous's gaze, her eyes twinkling, her voice breaking into a giggle. 'All those euros on a wedding, and one day when I get tired, when I stop liking him even a little... because I will one day...' She stopped, the twinkle in her eyes dimmed, the giggling gone. Her voice dropped. 'I will because my heart can only take so much, no? When that day comes, I'll tell him it's over.' She cleared her throat, shut her eyes and when she opened them, stars were dancing in them again. 'When the time comes, whether he has his papers or not, I'll tell him it's over. But right now, he'll do. It's fair, no?' She smiled again. 'And Prosperous?' She held Prosperous's gaze. 'I have a feeling that that day is soon. Very, very soon. There won't be time for him to have those papers!'

The air shifted in the kitchen and brought with it a sweet, pungent scent like the lingering smell of dry earth after a rain, the blood of gods.

Cleared for Takeoff

When I grow up, I'm going to be a teacher, Papa,' Bola told me as I walked her to school. 'But first, I have to be white, right?' The world stopped. She sounded so proud of herself that it broke my heart.

'Sweetie, you don't have to be white to be anything,' I said. Where was this coming from?

She put her arms on her waist and said earnestly, 'Of course you have to be white, Papa. Have you ever seen a black teacher?"

I came to Belgium to play football with a first division team. A knee injury two and a half years in ended that career and landed me in a small city in Flanders called Turnhout. With no university degree and not qualified for much else, and reluctant to return to Lagos, the manager of my club got me a job for life working in a furniture manufacturing factory owned by one of the football club's sponsors (and a route to be able to apply for Belgian citizenship for Ego and me). All the international players, once they were too injured or too old to play, were guaranteed a job for life there, unless they'd made enough money to never have to work again. I enjoyed working with my hands, the physical nature of my job meant that I did not have to worry about keeping fit, and the job was secure but that day, all I could hear as I heaved and assembled furniture was Bola's voice in my head saying she had to be white to be a teacher. The poverty of her imagination, more painful than the reality of it. There was not a single black teacher in her school, it was true. Or in any of the other schools around us in the city. I was haunted by all the other professions my daughter most likely thought precluded her for being black. She could not be a doctor (there were no black doctors in Turnhout). No black bankers (I took her sometimes to the bank with me). No black pharmacists (she had asked me once who the men and women in white coats were). I could not concentrate and once or twice, I let a tool slip. I needed to talk to Ego.

I was already playing professional football in Lagos when I met Ego. She was studying Chemical Engineering at the university then. When I got the chance to play for Anderlecht just after she graduated, and we had been married less than a year, she agreed to come with me. One of only three females in her entire graduating year, and the best graduating student, Ego was sure of a job with one of the top oil companies in Nigeria. 'I can get an engineering job anywhere but you can't play the level of football you want to here,' she told me when I wondered if it was fair of me to ask her to make such a big sacrifice. 'You, us, our marriage is my priority. What sort of wife would I be if I didn't support you? Or left you for the Belgium women?'

But she had left, after all, Ego. Left Bola and me.

A schoolmate of hers with whom she had reconnected
on Facebook had told her there was a shortage of good
teachers in London. Why was she wasting her brilliant
education in a factory? 'Just go online, look for openings
and apply!' the schoolmate said. London wasn't far, it
was practically next door. Ego could stay with her, see
what she thought of it. If it didn't work out, she could
always move back to Belgium. What did she have to
lose? Very little, Ego decided.

'See how well she looks!' she said to me, pointing the
woman out to me on her computer. She went through the
classmate's pictures of holidays in Bali and Disneyland,
Orlando with her children. 'She made a second class
lower, and she has a job as an engineer with a private
firm!' She tortured herself reading the woman's updates.
'I'm wasting away here!' she said. I didn't want her to go
but I knew how tempted she was, how the possibility of
living a life that came close to her classmate's expectations
of her lured her. I also knew that unlike me, she could
not stand to do the same repetitive thing that required
nothing of her but dexterity and the ability to stand on
her feet. The mindlessness of tagging packaged goods 9
hours a day numbed her.

'We could all move to London,' she said one night as
we were watching TV. Bola was in bed.

'How am I supposed to give up the job I have here
to go to London and start again? What's there for me
in London beside rain and fog?' Doing the same thing

over and over again for over 11 years gave me a level of comfort Ego did not understand. And I liked the city. Turnhout was quiet, the sort of city one could raise a child in without worrying about crime or the cost of housing. Healthcare was free (almost), education was free and childcare was affordable.

'So you don't mind if I go on my own then? Try it out? See what happens?'

But she was not the only educated one being forced to sacrifice, I said. Prosperous and Agu, did she think they didn't have degrees? Prosperous cleaned homes, and she hadn't left her husband yet. 'I'm not Prosperous,' she said. Yet, when anyone asked me if I didn't mind, I never admitted that I felt betrayed. I had no right to, I thought. Ego had given up a lot for me. I did not tell Ego she couldn't go (I couldn't) but a part of me wished that she would, as she had in the past, choose me (and Bola).

'This place is killing me,' she said the night before she left, already excited about the interviews she had lined up, the new job that would require the use of her brains. When she came back after the interviews, I could see we were already losing her. She complained about the cashier at C&A on the Gasthuisstraat who followed her around in the store, complained about the policeman who came into the call centre on De Merodelei asking for identity cards and ferrying off two men in their van, complained about stores closing on Sundays so she couldn't buy sanitary towels and had to wait until the next day. 'In London, stores are open every day!' she said.

In her first year in London, she came home when she had extended weekends and we went to see her those weekends she couldn't come. During the day, we went out into London. Trafalgar Square, Madam Tussaud's, four-year-old Bola between the two of us, bridging a crack that I could already see appearing. Ego looked different, glamorous almost. When she worked at the factory, she only dressed up on Sundays to go to church. Now, when she visited us or when Bola and I drove to London to see her, she dressed like someone out of a magazine. Red lipstick and high heeled shoes, skirts with slits and colourful sweaters. And always, she smelt of perfume. Bola and I looked out of place in her flat. Like we were puzzle pieces which no longer fit. When she talked of Ofsted and GCSEs and A*, I switched off. I didn't want to hear. There were times I wondered if I was not being childish but a still voice always reminded me that Ego broke us first. We should have been enough for her. One day, we had an argument and she said maybe if we had relocated to America or London or anywhere her devotion to love and family would not be tested by being made to work with her hands while her mind languished, we would not have to live apart. She had worked too hard for her degree to ever feel satisfied not being able to work without it . 'It's like having wings and not being able to fly. I tried, Gbolahan. I tried.'

'She deserves this,' I told them. 'I am Bola's father, I can look after her as well as Ego can. Besides we see her often, it's not like she's moved away and we never see her at all.' But no matter how hard I tried, that betrayal was a cancer that ate at me and then mutated into anger so I no longer wanted to drive down to London to see her with Bola. If she wanted to see us, let her make the effort! In Turnhout, I loved Bola for the two of us. I spoiled her like no child should be spoiled. I gave in and ordered her pizza as often as she wanted it. I took her to Bart Smit on the Gasthuistraat and let her squander my money on toys that had no durability. I took her to Panos on Saturday mornings for hot cocoa and waffles. Bola loved it. She lapped up the attention and the sweetness. She was a happy kid. And all this while, I thought now, feeling a sadness gather around me like water, she wanted to be white? She didn't think she was enough? Don't be silly, a voice inside me chided. *She wants to be a teacher, she doesn't want to be white.*

One day, on Bola's 5th birthday (which Ego had missed as it was on a school day), I told Ego on the phone that I didn't want Bola getting confused.

'Confused? How?'

'I don't want her going to see Mama in one country and Papa in another one. The best thing would be for you to come home or else...'

'Or else...'

From anybody else, it would have been a question, an invitation for me to complete my sentence, to issue my threat. But I knew Ego well enough to know that it was a challenge, inviting me to do my worst. Warning me that she would not budge. I should have known better than to give her an ultimatum. The "or else..." hung in

the air the entire day, sneaking into my nostrils, lying in
bed with me at night. It taunted me until I called Ego
while our daughter was asleep and put words to thoughts
that had been skirting around my mind for a long time.
Ego did not say she would return, she did not say she
would give up her job, she did not say that she was a bad
mother, putting her career before her family.

When I filed for divorce, I also asked for full custody.
If Ego did not want to live with her daughter, she could
not have her part-time. Ego did not contest the divorce.
She gave in so easily that my victory felt limp. I had to
find ways to make it count. If I did not break her, what
was the point? When she called one weekend to say she
could not have Bola because of a work commitment,
and tried to reschedule for the next weekend, I said 'No.
No. If you can't make it, you don't get another chance.' I
could not believe the cruelty I was capable of, but I could
not help it. A man scorned. Thin line between love and
hate and all that.

Now, as I drilled a hole into the back of a table I was
working on, I thought again of Ego teaching in London.
Giving her students wings to fly. And I thought of Bola
thinking she had to be white to be a teacher. Too young
to make the connection between what her mother did
and what she wanted to do. But not young enough to
notice that people like her, like her Papa, were not visible
in certain spaces. I wanted my daughter to dream. To fly.
I did not want her wings clipped before they'd even had

a chance to grow. It was almost time for my break. I went
outside to smoke.

I knew before I took out my phone that I was going
to call Ego. I knew before I said the words that I would
tell her that I was sorry, that I wanted her to have Bola,
to guard her wings, grow them out, to keep her safe in
a way that I could not here. 'I'll be visiting as often as I
can,' I said.

And maybe, that inner voice that constantly kept me
company said slyly, curling up the tip of my cigarette into
my ear, *maybe both of you will even have another chance.* I
did think of that. *You never stopped loving her, did you?* It's
probably too late for me. *Ja, you're right. You fucked up
big time.* I know. *She probably has someone else.* I flung the
half-smoked cigarette on the concrete floor and brought
judgment upon it: the heel of my shoe heavy over it,
stubbing it out, grinding it into the floor, silencing the
taunting voice.

Love of a Fat Woman

When Godwin brought his wife home to meet his family, his twin sisters hid their faces behind their hands and laughed. They said hello to their new sister-in-law and said, 'We are very happy to meet you.' Yet he could see the laughter bubbling underneath. Godwin had told them on the phone that she was not beautiful, but he had said nothing about either her corpulence or the fact that she smoked like a man.

'Could you not find anyone better?' his mother asked him later that night while the new wife slept in the bedroom Adaku and Oyilinneya had vacated on their mother's orders. Her snoring was deep and rhythmic, as if keeping count to some unheard music.

'She grunts like a pig,' he said. 'Sometimes I sleep on the sofa because her snoring keeps me awake.'

The mother looked at him and shook her head, the way she did when she saw images of starving children with bloated stomachs. Not with pity, but with something akin to bafflement that people survived such poverty.

'If she grew her hair, she might look better,' she said to Godwin.

'Perhaps,' Godwin agreed, rubbing his palms together, 'but I did not marry her for her looks.'

'Yes,' his mother agreed. 'But even then...' She sighed. 'You live with her. You see her every day. How do you stand it?'

Godwin shrugged.

His mother worried the beads around her wrist. Then she said, 'How do I show her off to the other women, eh?'

'You do not have to show her off at all,' Godwin snapped. She looked annoyed, so to placate her he said, 'I'll marry a nice woman for you. A woman who will give you lots of grandchildren.'

He had rung his ex, Kate, and she had been excited to hear from him. No, she was not yet married. Yes, she would love to meet up soon. If she was still as beautiful as he remembered, he would ask her to wait for him.

His mother smiled. 'When? When will you marry a proper wife?'

'When this is all over,' he said waving a hand over the deep, red couches of his mother's sitting room as if they were the "this" he meant.

He'd ordered the furniture earlier that day. The power it had given him to walk into a showroom and say, 'That set of two please,' and then have it delivered on the back of a truck. His mother had waited at the door, taking in the congratulations of neighbours who had trooped out to watch the men from the furniture shop offload the couches and carry them into the sitting room on the first floor. Then she followed them in and told them where to place them. No thank you, the plastic wrapping could stay.

The plastic sheeting squeaked with every movement but it did not bother his mother, who sat on each of the six cushions, bouncing softly to test them for comfort. 'How soft this velvet is,' she said, running a palm across the length of the armrests. Godwin asked her how long she was going to leave the cushions wrapped up for.

'My first set of new furniture in over thirty years and you think I am in a hurry to tear the plastic off? Biko, leave me, let me enjoy seeing them like this!'

Whatever he did, he did for his mother. She had been uppermost in his mind that night at the club in Antwerp when he smiled back at the first white girl to smile at him. The girl was not his type, but he could see the potential in her. If he played his cards right, she could help him become the sort of man he had dreamt of being: the sort of man who could finally repay his mother for the years of sacrifice she'd endured and grant her an early retirement from her petty trading, which no longer brought in as much as it used to. And even then it had not brought in nearly enough. Three mouths to feed and a husband disposed of by cholera; he had never known his mother to stop and rest. It thrilled him now to see her sit on the couch, her legs spread out in front of her, twirling a brand-new handbag. Tine had chosen the bag herself, her present for *mijn schoonmama*!

Godwin had no sharp recollection of his father. That is to say that what he remembered was vague, a liquid shadow as if seen through the rain, walking out of the door every morning with a battered briefcase and a bowler hat on his head. Both the briefcase and the bowler hat had

been kept for him, preserved in a paper bag on top of
the wardrobe in his mother's bedroom. When he was
younger, not so young as to be scared by the thought
of wearing a dead man's hat, but young enough to be
sentimental about his meagre inheritance, he would
climb on a chair to reach the top of the cupboard, bring
down the paper bag and bury his head in the hat, taking
in huge gulps of his father's scent. The memory warmed
him and he felt happiness like molten lava flow through
his veins. He smiled.

'What are you smiling at?' his mother asked.

'Just happy to be home.'

He had not expected to miss Nigeria when he left. First
he went to Cyprus, because it was easier to get into. And
cheaper. And he had had been promised by the agent
who got him the visa that he would be able to work on a
farm. He had indeed worked for a sturdy farmer whose
name he could not pronounce. He was worked like a
horse, but he was fed. And he had a room in which to
dream. He had made his way from Cyprus to Spain and
then to Belgium, where he was determined to become a
legal resident. He was tired of wondering when he would
be caught and deported. He went into clubs that would
let him in without an ID and smiled into the faces of
young girls, who mainly ignored him or scowled. When
he met Tine, he held onto her. She was his passport.

When she whispered her fears to him at night—that
she was fat, needed to lose weight to keep his love—he
touched her breasts and told her that he had never fallen
for skinny girls. 'I like my women with fat on them, baby,

and you are just perfect.' Lying was easy if you kept your
eye on the goal. She often asked him to tell his version
of when they met. 'I could not keep my eyes off you,' he
told her.

'And what was the first thing you said to me?' Tine
liked to ask, clearly relishing the game.

'I asked if it hurt when you fell from heaven because
for sure you were an angel.'

It was a cheesy line, but he couldn't think of anything
better and it had sent Tine into shrieks of laughter. She
looked almost pretty when she laughed, eyes shining and
mouth spread wide, exposing soft pink gums.

And that was the beginning of their love affair. He
asked her to marry him within months and, even though
she said she was young, and it was too soon and shouldn't
they get to know each other better? She accepted and
threw herself into the preparations, harassing city officials,
who questioned Godwin's motives, and handling the
rigmarole of the marriage process until the road was
cleared and they could marry.

She danced like a whirlwind at the wedding—which set
him back a fair bit—and proclaimed that it was the very
best day of her life. It was the best day of his too. He
had a marriage certificate and a whole life of legalised
stay in Europe ahead of him. Once he got his Belgian
citizenship, it would be thank you and bye-bye to Tine.
Sometimes, not often, he felt a twinge of guilt but what
was he doing wrong, really? It wasn't like she was not
getting anything out of it. He was giving her a huge ego
boost. She liked to show him off to her friends. Really,
it was a fair deal.

It was not part of the deal to come back to Nigeria so soon on holiday but he had had no choice. Tine had wanted to meet his family and he had to keep her sweet until he got what he wanted. So here they were, his mother asking if Tine was the best he could do and his younger sisters giggling behind her back, mimicking her waddle and her cigarette smoking. He had to remind them that, had he waited until he found Miss Belgium, he might have been found out and deported, and then where would they all be, eh? That killed the giggles.

He loved his sisters, Adaku and Oyilinneya. Fifteen and beautiful, they would have no problems getting good husbands when the time came. He was giving them a good education, providing them with a comfortable home. They did not have to hawk bread as he had done to help make ends meet. After everything he had been through, he was entitled to a break. And if he were honest with himself, there was a lot to like about Tine. There were times he thought that, had he met her under different circumstances, had he not been focused on making sure that he had the right papers to stay on in Belgium, he could have loved her. Granted, she was bigger than the type of women he fell for, but there were times when he put his head between her breasts and never wanted to stir. There was also a confidence about her, when she was not complaining to him about her weight, that he found sexy. She walked into rooms as as if they were hers. And she was compassionate, one of the most compassionate people he knew, a trait that had influenced her choice of career.

Tine was a woman of little frivolity, which was what one might expect of someone who spent her days working in an old people's home. Her only excess was the wedding. She had told him she wanted a Nigerian wedding. *My Big Fat Nigerian wedding,* she said. She had not contributed a cent to it. Godwin worked in a factory and enjoyed his beer, but Tine said they had to save, adding her salary to what he earned so that they could build up a fortune for whatever children they would have. She calculated how much they would save if he cut down from three bottles of beer a night to one. She meticulously cut out supermarket coupons from newspapers, and scoured aisles for bargains on washing powder and shampoo. He was grateful, he really was.

'Nigeria is going to cost a lot!' Godwin had told Tine when she first suggested the holiday. When she was not put off by all the inoculations he told her she would need, was not put off by the fear of contracting malaria from vicious mosquitoes, he had hoped that an appeal to her frugality would do the trick. But she had said, 'We have savings, schat. Take it from the joint account. I want to see your family. This is important to me.'

The days in Enugu moved like an overfed dog, and darkness came early, as if the days themselves could not wait to go to sleep. Tine asked to see the city, so Godwin took her to the new burger and pizza joints his sisters feverishly spoke about and where he was sure not to run into anyone who knew him. They took his sisters along and the girls enjoyed their food despite Godwin saying that the pizza was nothing but stew on bread, and nothing at all like the pizzas of Europe. Tine smoked and asked if they could not go anywhere more "authentic".

When she complained that his sisters hardly spoke to her, he said it was because they were shy. When she complained of his mother not exchanging a word with her—*She seems almost uncomfortable in my presence*—Godwin said it was because his mother spoke no English. Tine said she could not wait to go back to Belgium; the vacation was not what she had expected. Godwin did not dispute that. She moved around listlessly, smoking on the balcony, complaining of the heat and retiring to the bedroom to sleep long before anyone else went to bed.

The second week of their stay—halfway into the vacation—Godwin's grandmother arrived from the village smelling of the earth and carrying a sack of almonds and mangoes dirtied with sand. She wore thick glasses and asked in a loud voice for "the new wife". She had not been told that Tine was not a real wife, just a woman Godwin had married to get his papers, and now Godwin felt guilty at her enthusiasm. He sent for Tine, who came out of the room in a sleeveless baby-pink dress, her face and arms flushed, putting Godwin in mind of a giant pig.

'*Mijn oma,*' Godwin said dully, introducing his grandmother to Tine.

Tine mumbled 'Hello,' but the old woman spread her arms and made rapid movements like a bird flapping its wings. Tine stood where she was, looking into the woman's face with a puzzled expression.

Godwin's grandmother took the few steps needed to bridge the gap between them and hugged Tine. She held her and spoke Igbo into her ears, words that Tine surely could make no sense of. She let go of Tine, smiled at the room and said, 'Ah, our Godwin has brought us back a real woman! A beautiful woman. Her skin shines like a polished wall.'

Godwin looked at Tine and thought, *Yes, her skin does shine!* And how had he never noticed that her short hair suited her, the red at its tip like tongues of fire complementing her baby-pink dress. He watched his grandmother trace Tine's face, proclaim again how beautiful "our new wife" is and lead Tine by the hand to the sitting room.

She handed the sack of fruit to Adaku to be washed and asked that a plate of mangoes be brought to the sitting room. She was going to sit down and eat them with her new granddaughter.

For the rest of the day, she sat with Tine in the sitting room, eating mangoes, Tine copying the old woman, cupping her chin with her left hand the same way the woman did to catch the juice dripping from the fruit. His grandmother spoke in Igbo and Tine spoke in Flemish and they both laughed that they could not understand each other, and when the grandmother pointed to the plastic sheet on the sofa and mimicked the act of tearing it off, Tine laughed and her laughter tinkled a bell and at that moment Godwin felt a stirring, something tender that he thought might be the beginning of love.

How to Survive a
Heat Wave

Outside, the weather is changing. Autumn is colouring leaves red, purple and gold. It is cold but not yet cold enough for the heaters to come on. Inside, it is sweltering. Añuli's guests have peeled off their scarves and their coats and their sweaters. Only Añuli is still in a thick sweater, despite how high she has set the heating. The three women are huddled around a table, a large tray of unshelled melon seeds in the centre of it, and beside it, a bowl for the shelled seeds. Nina Simone is playing on the stereo:

You took my teeth....
But it is finished because I'm too wise...

'The thing about this place,' Añuli says above the music, 'is that there are too many options. It gets people confused. Even ordinary bread: there are so many types to choose from! I just stood there like a zombie!'

This is not really what she wants to say. She wants to say something else but it is easier, at the moment, to speak of being bombarded with options in Europe, to speak of standing in front of the bread aisle in Carrefour and not knowing which of the different types to pick.

She does not tell them that she has never had this problem before, befuddled by bread, or that these days, her morning begins in the middle of the night when she gets up and can no longer sleep. Or that all this started with the incident on the train (about which they know nothing).

True, her friends nod, helping her to shell the melon seeds her aunt sent from Nigeria through someone who returned recently.

'Why did this woman send you unshelled egusi sef?' Oge complains. 'She could have had it shelled and ground at so little cost. Who sends unshelled egusi to someone abroad?'

'See?' Añuli says. 'This place spoils you. Back home, we wouldn't have thought anything of shelling melon seeds. This is a place of choice and convenience. You want pounded yam? You buy it powdered. You want spinach? You buy it washed and chopped.'

She scooped up a handful of egusi. 'This isn't so bad. Sitting here, doing this together... community. This—' she stops because her voice is already breaking.

'Yes, we would have shelled them—' Oge presses on.

'Or our maids would have,' Prosperous interrupts.

'And back home we would have handpicked the stones out of rice,' Oge continues. 'But this is not back home, is it? Back home you'd have many hands to help. You'd have had a multitude of maids. If we hadn't come, you'd have had to do this all alone.'

'Take religion,' Añuli continues. She is glad her friends do not notice that she was, just then, on the verge of tears. She has not really been paying attention to Oge. It is hard enough for her to concentrate on not letting the wrong words rush out. 'Back home, people are either believers or heathen. Believers or infidels, if one is in the north.'

Before they came here, she did not know it was possible to be anything other than those, she says. Here, she has met humanists and atheists (who she has been told are different from unbelievers, but she can no longer remember how). There are witches, not like the witches of back home, who were to be feared and who turned to bats at night, but normal-looking women who pose for photographs in lifestyle magazines like *Flair* and *Libelle*. You can be anything, but not heathen.

'You know my friend, Lies? I asked her once why there are no heathens here. "Heathen? What is that? Is that African?" she said.'

The women laugh.

'Lies's name na wah!' Añuli says and her friends laugh again. They know where this is going. 'The first time I saw it spelled, I said, "That's English. Laaiz!" I was joking but Lies said, "No. It's pronounced leez. Very Flemish."'

That is how Lies explains everything. It's very Flemish. Macaroni with ham and cheese, which she encourages Añuli to try, is very Flemish. The rice pudding she offers her, which Añuli thinks is a travesty, is very Flemish. Her loneliness is very Flemish. What would Lies say, she wonders now, about the incident on the train?

Lies is a humanist, which means she believes in the human spirit. 'And what if the human spirit is evil?' Añuli asked her once.

'The human spirit is essentially good,' Lies replied. 'Circumstances make them bad.' She did not understand what Lies meant, nor was she sure Lies completely understood what she meant either.

Some people were born bad and neither circumstance nor environment could account for their badness. That's what her mother always said. How else could you account for some of the wicked things people did? The mother who strangled her own baby? The slave trade? Colonisation? King Leopold in the Congo who had his men chop off the limbs of workers who underperformed? Those young men yesterday on the train from Herentals who violated her? She feels her hands shake still as she grabs another handful of egusi to peel.

'Did you hear about the Belgian woman who was under house arrest in Cuba?' Oge asks. 'She was on TV yesterday. With her Cuban husband and their son.'

'No,' Añuli says. She drags her mind back from the train.

'Well, so this woman was sentenced to house arrest for manslaughter.'

'Who did she kill?' Añuli asks.

'I don't know. I think a cyclist. Anyway, she comes back to Belgium after three years and talks about how she missed her parents, and her country and her frietjes met mayo!'

'Three years only?' Añuli asks and the women burst into laughter. Añuli has not been back in eight years. Prosperous in five, during which time her father died.

Three years does not sound long enough to miss anything. Three years is not a long enough sentence for killing anyone. It's not a long enough sentence for any kind of violation. Añuli feels a clamping in her chest. If she cries, she has to tell her friends everything and she is not yet ready to. She has not even told her husband. When she came home last night and made straight for the bathroom, she had told him she ate something which upset her stomach. He had rubbed her back while she threw up, brought her ginger tea in bed to soothe her stomach and yet, every time she began to talk to him about it, other words came out. Like now. The heavy words refuse to roll off her tongue. When she sent for Oge and Prosperous, her two best friends, she thought she would be able to tell them about it, get the mountain off her chest so that she could breathe better. But once they arrived, the unholy trifecta of fear, humiliation and shame blocked the words. Instead, she had brought out the melon seeds and told them, 'Ngwa, we have an egusi peeling party here!'

She wants them to keep talking, anything to keep her from reliving the events: the carriage that stank of beer that should have warned her, the half a dozen young men, young enough that she could have given birth to them, singing riotously in it, waving to her as she got in and seated herself near an older white woman. They appeared to be university students going home for the weekend to have their laundry done. The woman she was seated beside teased them about it. In Tielen, the woman got off. No one else got in.

'Come sit with us! Have a beer on us,' one of the men waved her over as the train doors closed and the train hurtled off towards Turnhout. *The end station. Station Turnhout.*

'No, thank you.' She had sent a smile their way, touched by their friendliness. She might have thought, *To be young again.* To be carefree and happy. Not to have to think about bills or house rent or holidays back to your country which you can't afford. She and her husband, Ifedi have been saving to be able to move back to Nigeria once their twins, still in third grade, enter secondary school.

'You're too good for us?' The one who had offered the beer was now sitting opposite her, his voice no longer as friendly. He slammed the beer on the table between them. 'Drink!' His mates laughed and began chanting, *Drink! Drink! Drink!*

Añuli ignored him and brought out her phone. She hoped he would go back to his seat. That his friends would stop egging him on. She was starting to feel uncomfortable. She wished the conductor would pass through but she knew from experience that at that time of the night and with under nine minutes to the train's final destination, it was unlikely to happen. The train was almost empty and she had chosen this carriage precisely because there were other people in it. It was common sense, she always thought, to sit in a carriage with other passengers, people who could help you if you needed help, strength in numbers.

What happened next, happened quickly. She remembers the phone falling from her hands. She remembers standing up and heading for the door. She remembers being blocked from reaching the door. She remembers her shouting swallowed up by the men's chanting. She remembers hands grabbing her breasts. Feeling under her skirt. She remembers screaming. She remembers the men, beer cans in hand disappearing into the night once the train stopped in Turnhout. She remembers their laughter still haunting her long after they'd left the train and she had begun to make the walk home from the station.

'You know Joke, the woman I clean for? She thinks people should not kill animals.' Prosperous says.

Oge hisses. 'That Joke has never known hunger. Only people who have never known hunger can talk like that.'

'She says it's immoral.' Prosperous says. 'We had a neighbour in Enugu who had a dog called Spaniel. They thought they were oyibo, the way they spoilt this animal, eh! The daughter of the woman told me once that Spaniel would not eat any food left for it on the floor; it had to be in its bowl. She told me how they had dog biscuits and powdered milk especially for the dog. One day, Spaniel bit a visitor, someone important, a chief or something, who had come to see the man of the house. Ha! The woman gave Spaniel to their gateman.'

'Ah ah? What did they want the gateman to do with the dog?' Oge pours all the shelled egusi into a tray.

'Ha!' Prosperous says. 'The gateman was Calabar. Spaniel went into his pepper soup that night.'

'A 404 special!' Oge says.

'Do you blame the poor man?' Añuli asks. 'It would be like giving an Igbo man a goat and asking him to keep it as a pet!'

'The woman regretted it later sha. Her daughter said the woman cried for many days that she missed Spaniel. She even fired the gateman for eating the dog!'

'That's unfair,' Oge hisses. 'What did she want the man to do? Hang onto the dog as a pet? Crazy woman!'

'But that's how the rich treat the poor. There's nothing fair about it,' Añuli says. There are many other things that are not fair, she thinks. She is cold and cannot stop the shivering. Her friends have asked her if she has a fever. 'Coming down with a little something', she lied. Her skin is raw from her scrubbing it in the tub, wanting to leave nothing of the old behind. She recollects Lies telling her that in Belgium, rape is not considered a violent crime but a moral one. Yet each time those men on the train touched her, it felt as if they were lacerating her. What happened to her on the train was violent. She had come home and locked herself in the bathroom.

She thinks of Nwadiuto, her school mate at the University of Ilorin who killed herself after the rumour went round that she was raped in the male hostel. Añuli wasn't friends with Nwadiuto but she knew her well enough to say hello when they bumped into each other, which was often as they were in the same hall. Yet, when the news broke about the rape, she remembers asking, like so many others, why the girl had gone to the male hostel. *And at night! What was she expecting?*

The student who raped her had a reputation, apparently

for sexually assaulting women, so why did Nwadiuto agree to meet him in his room? *She should have known better! Everyone knows this, never meet a guy in his room alone unless you're asking for wahala!* A few weeks later when the news of Nwadiuto's suicide spread, Añuli had not understood why, had not understood the depth of despair that anyone could get to, to tie a scarf around their neck and hang themselves. She heard later that Nwadiuto's parents had been too ashamed of how their daughter died to have a proper funeral for her, *No guests, just a quick service with their family only.*

'And who can blame them?' Añuli recalls asking now.

'In the olden days,' another student said, 'suicide victims were thrown away. They weren't even buried!'

The memory of Nwadiuto that she has buried so deep inside her, so deep that in all the years since her suicide, she never thought of the girl once, excavates itself and she can remember the girl in startling detail. The remembrance brings her pain. Her body is heating up. She pulls off her sweater.

'What's wrong?' Oge and Prosperous ask almost in unison.

Añuli opens her mouth and the words that could not come out before begin to spill out, spreading out in the room, mingling with her pool of tears, releasing the clamp in her chest, relieving her of that unholy trifecta. And from her stereo, Simone is still belting out, *But it is finished because I'm too wise.*

Heart Is Where
The Home Is

I missed my mother. This missing was not an abstract thing but a palpable object, an exaggerated Adam's apple that threatened to choke me every time I swallowed. It had crept up on me sometime in my first year overseas, a slight ball of wool that bothered me now and then but after three years it had become unbearable. When I came back from work and had no one to talk to, when I shopped for one and cooked for one, and sat in front of my TV eating the food alone, I missed her. The day I bought a mango and remembered how, in elementary school, we had cracked open mango seeds to look for the hidden earrings urban legend said were in them, I missed not being able to laugh about it with my mother.

When a colleague suggested that I might be homesick, I told her not to be silly. It was not homesickness that weighed on me but my mother's absence. Besides, this was my home. Belgium. And I wanted my mother here.

It might have helped if I'd had friends, people to fill my house and lounge about on my chairs but I had neither the time nor the inclination to invest in making new friends. I used to be a shy child, unable to make friends easily, but I had not minded it. As an adult, I have never really cared to make friends. My mother used to ask me all the time as a teenager, when the same one or two friends came to visit, *Ndi, don't you have other friends you want to visit? (No). Don't you miss not having a large group of friends? (No).* Now in Belgium, I did not seek the company of fellow Africans or of my colleagues outside of work. No friend would have filled the empty space I wanted my mother to occupy. My home was incomplete without her. It had always been the two of us.

My father had died when I was eight. The day he died, I came back from school to find my mother wailing and rolling on our veranda. That day, my mother was not left alone on the veranda to cry. Four of her friends were there, watching over her like guardian angels, crying with her. They were the ones who remembered that I needed lunch, and who forced my mother to eat.

I was twenty-four when I left home for the first time. Unlike many of the girls I went to primary school with, I had not gone on to boarding school, even though I had passed the entrance examination to Queens College, one of the top secondary schools in the country. I applied to a university a taxi ride away.

Most people swear that daughters and mothers cannot live together for so long without suffocating each other. With my mother and me, it was the opposite. We were close, but it was a closeness that gave us room to breathe. In between perms, my mother still braided my hair. I told her about my classes. She knew the names of all my professors, knew that one had a habit of beginning every class with a prayer, knew of another who looked so young she was often mistaken for a student herself. She knew that I liked my Chem 201 professor because she was possibly the smartest person I had ever come across.

My mother was vivacious while I, although no longer shy, preferred friendships in small doses. I did not have more than a few friends at a time, and often not for very long. I knew my mother would have liked me to have more friends, but she never pushed me. Perhaps her friends filled the house enough for the two of us. And she was enough for me.

Even before I left the country, I told my mother that, once I was settled, I wanted her to move in with me. Within three months of living in Belgium, I begged her with every phone call (at least once a week) to come and live with me. I promised her a rest from days of sitting in the sun selling peppers and tomatoes to customers determined to pay the lowest price possible. I had a good job now. It was my responsibility to make life easier for her. After all her hard work, she could reap the benefits, spend her days in my air-conditioned home and rest her feet on a side table in my sitting room. I imagined coming home from work to eat with her. Weekends, we could go shopping together. I would rent Nollywood films for us to watch together.

I was at the airport a full hour before her flight was scheduled to arrive. I sat at a table by myself and drank coffee while I waited, watching people come and go, imagining all the things that I would soon be able to do with my mother. When I saw her she looked startled. It reminded me of my own wide-eyed wonder at the gleaming smoothness of the airport floor three years ago. This woman with her wig covering one eye looked nothing like the mother I remembered. She looked older. Unkempt. Ordinary. Not a hint of redness on her lips.

The mother of my memories was elegant. She would not step out of the house without red lipstick and perfect hair. She did not walk with slow steps as this stranger did. This was not the mother who told me that, no matter how hard life got, a woman owed it to herself to dress well. The mother who, despite the poverty my father's death and his brothers' greed had driven us to, always managed to look glamorous.

It took her a while to notice me. I waved, she waved back, her face breaking into a smile. And then I ran to her. She smelled the same. At least that had not changed. I held her and soaked in her scent the way I did as a child when I woke up from a nightmare in which she was killed in a car accident, the way my father had been. I fought the urge to straighten her wig. I hugged her and the familiar warmth of her dissolved whatever shock I felt at her deterioration.

'You look tired,' I said, taking over her luggage trolley.

'I have not slept in twenty-four hours.'

'Why not? I especially booked a night flight for you so you'd be well rested.'

'I could not sleep on the plane. I haven't seen my own daughter in three years. Was I going to risk missing my stop?'

My mother had never been on an aeroplane but it had not occurred to me that she would think that planes operated like the buses she took from Nsukka to Lagos. Although I wanted to laugh, I did not want her to think that I was ridiculing her. I was consoled in thinking that perhaps her ageing was temporary, caused by lack of sleep, and that once she had rested she would revert to the woman I remembered. She held my hand in both of hers and I knew that she too had missed me.

My mother's startled look lingered throughout the first week after her arrival. Her gaze lighted upon my doorknobs *(shiny)*; my TV *(big)*; the rug *(soft, soft like a baby blanket)*; the fruit basket *(These bananas look plastic)*; the neighbour across the street who shouted a greeting in Flemish and I responded *(How did you ever learn this language?)*.

At the end of the first week, she set her gaze on me and said, 'This house is too quiet. How come you never have visitors? Have you no friends?'

'Of course I do!'

'So how come they do not come here?'

'Because everyone's busy.'

'Doing?'

'Working.'

She clucked her tongue against her teeth the same way she did when I told her at sixteen that the boy she had caught me with was just a classmate.

While I was out at work, my mother divided her time between cooking and watching TV. I was glad I had cable so that, when the local Belgian channels did not air programmes in English, she could always depend on the BBC stations and CNN. My home smelled of my childhood: okra soup and jollof rice; yam pottage and beans. I could close my eyes and be the precarious eight-year-old on her father's knees, while her mother dished out food in deep porcelain bowls.

Not even those bowls had survived my uncles' greedy hands. The car was the first to go, the Peugeot 504 in which we had driven to church on Sunday mornings. Uncle Justus, my father's older brother, laid claim to that. As he did the sofas, the TV and finally the house.

My tenth birthday was spent helping my mother set up what was left of our belongings in a one-room flat, smaller than the bedroom she and my father had shared only two years before. As we unpacked, she made me promise that I would study hard, do well at school, and get a good job, so that no matter what happened to my husband in the future, I would be OK. I gave her my promise quickly, mortified by the thought of marriage. In that one room, my mother entertained her friends. Once a month, she hosted six women from her Christian Mothers' Group. On those days, they sat on the veranda, and kept me awake with their laughter.

'This is like being back home.'

'What is?'

'The smell of all the food you're cooking.'

My mother said, 'Nobody here speaks English!' as if the thought had just occurred to her. I saw the startled look in her eyes get wider.

Five weeks into her stay, she complained that she was running out of food. Was there any place where we could replenish her stocks? She had come with bags of ground egusi and dried bitter-leaf; ground crayfish and smoked fish. I was amazed that customs had let her through with so much food. She said nobody checked.

'Why did you bring so much?' I asked the day she arrived.

'I was not sure I could stomach whatever it was you ate here. Mama Patience who went to visit her grandchildren in America warned me about the food. One does not learn a new dance in old age.'

'But this is not America, Mama. This is Belgium.'

'Belgium. America. Obodo oyibo is obodo oyibo.'

On a sunny Saturday afternoon, I took my mother to an African supermarket in Antwerp. When the shopkeeper said to her in English, 'Hello, Mama,' my mother's response was effusive. She asked him where he was from.

'Ghana is Nigeria's sister,' my mother said before asserting the superiority of Nigerian jollof rice over Ghana's version. It was the most I had heard her say in weeks.

The shopkeeper's response, which I did not catch, made my mother laugh. That was when it hit me. This was the first time she had laughed since her arrival. She had smiled. She had complimented. But she had not laughed. That day at the supermarket, everything set her off. I walked beside her. She picked up a guava, pinched it, smelled it, laughed and threw it in the shopping trolley. At that moment, her laughter gleaming in her eyes, I realised that I had unwittingly dragged her to museums and malls to dazzle her into letting out the mirth that had earned her the nickname Joy. In her first week with me, I took days off and accompanied her around Belgium. We went to the zoo in Antwerp, we took a horse carriage ride in Ghent, we went on the tourist bus in Brussels and took pictures in front of the palace, but she did not seem entertained. We took the train to Bruges and walked to the Boudewijn Theme Park and Dolfinarium. We caught a dolphin show and she wondered aloud how an animal that looked so dumb could be as intelligent as to dance in sync with humans. She asked if we were single-handedly supporting the place when, at her insistence, I told her how much our tickets had cost. She had gone with me from one part of the theme park to the other but nothing had amused her. I did not see in her eyes the same enthusiasm that I'd felt the first time I visited the park.

After we came back from shopping, my mother sang as she cooked. Back in Nsukka, she would have been chatting with the neighbours. As a teenager who liked to spend time alone, I remember thinking that the only time my mother was ever truly alone was when she was in the bathroom. She sought company. If nobody came to visit, she went and visited them. As a first-year psychology student, I was certain that my father's death gave my mother a fear of being left alone. When I asked her about it, she said that the world was made to be enjoyed in company.

My mother's laughter lasted exactly two months. It was a generous, capacious laughter that accommodated even the most ridiculous: Judge Judy's tight smile on daytime

TV. *This Judge woman looks like she's being forced to smile with a lemon in her mouth, hahahaha!* The fact that, in this country, you did not just turn up at people's doorsteps. You waited to be invited. *Hahahaha!*

And then, just as it had showered upon my house, the laughter dried up. As did her voice. She hardly spoke to me. No longer asked if I had no friends. No longer marvelled at all the shiny things my home had to offer. She no longer played with the TV remote control trying to find programmes that interested her, mostly American and British soaps on cable and the news. She sat with me as I listened to the news in Dutch and muttered, 'I could never learn this language!' One day, she held her throat dramatically and said, 'This is what it must feel like to be dumb. To hear and not understand. To speak and not be understood.'

When we went out, she no longer said anything about the number of new cars on the roads. The house became a tomb, too sturdily built for me to crack open with my own voice. My mother looked sad, and her sadness permeated the house so that it seemed as if it, too, was in mourning. The doorknobs seemed to have lost the lustre my mother had so admired. No matter what she cooked it smelled of the incense she sometimes burned in our parlour back in Nigeria. Often I asked her what was wrong. Each time she told me it was nothing. The sadness wound itself around my ankles, slowing my usual quick strides. I began to wish that I had never asked her to come.

One day I came back from work and my mother was sobbing and rolling on the floor of the sitting room.

There were no friends crying with her as they had the day my father died. She had never been without friends. I had not managed to make a single friend here. I was not part of the Nigerian community because, in addition to my reclusive nature, my job kept me busy. I chatted to colleagues but never invited anyone home for a coffee. I had no desire to be inundated with people for whom I would have to be responsible: offering biscuits and drinks, keeping the conversation going. What I missed was the undemanding presence of a friend for whom I did not have to bear the social responsibilities of a hostess. Perhaps what I missed was not so much my mother but the company of a close friend.

I rolled close to my mother and held her tight. I held her until we both stopped crying. She got up, wiped her eyes and went into her bedroom. I did not follow. I did not ask what was wrong. I sat at my computer and booked her a ticket home.

Acknowledgements

I am grateful to all the wonderful people who spurred this book on by asking the right questions, providing coffee and wine and space; those who allowed me to pester them into reading early drafts; those who kept me sane with long phone calls and pep talks when I ran the risk of coming apart: Kate Johnson, agent and early reader; Bibi Bakare-Yusuf; Brian Chikwava; Elnathan John; Adamu Abubakar; Jude Dibia; Ike Ilegbune; Andrew Colarusso; Uwem Akpan; Kola Tubosun; Aruni Kashyap; all the editors who worked on this.

DW Gibson and Ledig House; Bill Pierce and Jennifer Alise Drew for publishing *Finding Faith* in AGNI; EC Osondu for that journey.

Jane, Winnie, Vic, Maureen, Okey and BG., siblings like no other; my parents for whom everything I write is worth celebrating.

My Jan and our boys-to-men.

More Cassava Shorts

Nights of the Creaking Bed
Toni Kan

ISBN: 978-1-911115-84-7

Nights of the Creaking Bed is full of colourful characters involved in affecting dramas: a girl who is rejected in love because she has three brothers to look after; a middle aged housewife who finds love again but has an impossible decision to make; a young man who can't get the image of his naked, beautiful mother out of his mind; a child so poor he has to hawk onions on Christmas day—and many others. Some, initially full of hope, find their lives blighted by the cruelty of others, or by being in the wrong place at the wrong time, or by just not knowing the "right" people.

The Whispering Trees
Abubakar Adam Ibrahim

ISBN: 978-1-911115-86-1

The magical tales in *The Whispering Trees* capture the essence of life, death and coincidence in Northern Nigeria. Myth and reality intertwine in stories featuring political agitators, newly-wedded widows, and the tormented whirlwind, Kyakkyawa. The two medicine men of Mazade battle against their egos, an epidemic and an enigmatic witch. And who is Okhiwo, whose arrival is heralded by a pair of little white butterflies?

Support *Better Late Than Never*

We hope you enjoyed reading this book. It was brought to you by Cassava Republic Press, an award-winning independent publisher based in Abuja and London. If you think more people should read this book, here's how you can help:

Recommend it. Don't keep the enjoyment of this book to yourself; tell everyone you know. Spread the word to your friends and family.

Review, review review. Your opinion is powerful and a positive review from you can generate new sales. Spare a minute to leave a short review on Amazon, GoodReads, Wordery, our website and other book buying sites.

Join the conversation. Hearing somebody you trust talk about a book with passion and excitement is one of the most powerful ways to get people to engage with it. If you like this book, talk about it, Facebook it, Tweet it, Blog it, Instagram it. Take pictures of the book and quote or highlight from your favourite passage. You could even add a link so others know where to purchase the book from.

Buy the book as gifts for others. Buying a gift is a regular activity for most of us—birthdays, anniversaries, holidays, special days or just a nice present for a loved one for no reason… If you love this book and you think it might resonate with others, then please buy extra copies!

Get your local bookshop or library to stock it. Sometimes bookshops and libraries only order books that they have heard about. If you loved this book, why not ask your librarian or bookshop to order it in. If enough people request a title, the bookshop or library will take note and will order a few copies for their shelves.

Recommend a book to your book club. Persuade your book club to read this book and discuss what you enjoy about the book in the company of others. This is a wonderful way to share what you like and help to boost the sales and popularity of this book. You can also join our online book club on Facebook at Afri-Lit Club to discuss books by other African writers.

Attend a book reading. There are lots of opportunities to hear writers talk about their work. Support them by attending their book events. Get your friends, colleagues and families to a reading and show an author your support.

Thank you!

Stay up to date with the latest books, special offers and exclusive content with our monthly newsletter.

Sign up on our website:
www.cassavarepublic.biz

Twitter: @cassavarepublic
Instagram: @cassavarepublicpress
Facebook: facebook.com/CassavaRepublic
Hashtag: #BetterNeverThanLate #ReadCassava

Transforming a manuscript into the book you are now reading is a team effort. Cassava Republic Press would like to thank everyone who helped in the production of *Better Never Than Late:*

Editorial
Lauren Smith
Bibi Bakare-Yusuf
Layla Mohamed

Design & Production
Seyi Adegoke

Sales & Marketing
Emma Shercliff
Kofo Okunola